THE SPIDER:
SCOURGE OF THE BLACK LEGIONS

MASTER OF MEN!

THE SPIDER®

SCOURGE OF THE BLACK LEGIONS

By Grant Stockbridge

POPULAR PUBLICATIONS • 2022

PUBLISHING HISTORY

"Scourge of the Black Legions" originally appeared in the November 1938 (Vol. 16, No. 2) issue of *The Spider* magazine. Copyright 2022 by Argosy Communications, Inc. All rights reserved.

CHAPTER 1
WHISPER OF DOOM

A DOUBLE file of policemen stood, back to back, and formed a narrow aisle from the doors of police headquarters to the powerful sedan waiting, with motor idling, at the curb. Each of the men held a revolver in his fist. On the buttresses, at either side of the doors, other men stood with machine guns. The eyes of all quested ceaselessly over the street, over the windows of the flanking buildings.

The doors whipped open and a chevroned sergeant barked an order at the police. "Close in!"

They narrowed the space between their backs so that a single man, with difficulty, could squeeze between them. The man in the doorway paused an instant. His face was lined with fatigue and his eyes, deep-set and shadowed, burned feverishly. He jerked his head impatiently at the tall, soldierly man beside him.

"Damn it, Kirk," he said irritably. "All this protection isn't necessary. If anyone wanted to kill me…."

"Some one apparently does," broke in the soldierly man— Stanley Kirkpatrick, revolutionary acting commissioner of police. His eyes swiftly swept the street and he nodded approval at the sergeant. "There have been two attempts on your life in the last forty-eight hours, Dick," he went on quietly. "It's madness for you even to leave headquarters."

"Let me be the judge of that, Kirk," the other man answered.

"Those poor people are calling for Richard Wentworth and if I don't show myself, they're likely to get out of control. You don't want five thousand victims of the plague roaming the streets, spreading the disease...."

Wentworth's lips snapped grimly shut. Forty-eight hours before, he had led his small force of outlawed men against the criminals who ruled New York City and had managed to seize a partial control. Those criminals were the ones who had spread this horrible, leprosy-like disease among the populace. There had been only Wentworth and his small body of men to fight against the tyrants. Now the stricken were appealing to him for relief from the plague. Great armies of disease-ridden people were marching toward the city for the injections which would cure them. The supplies were here and, given time, they would be treated. But meantime, they must be held outside city limits lest millions of others become infected....

"At least let me go in your place," Kirkpatrick made a final appeal. "Others can do my work, but we can't afford to lose you. Why, even this pilgrimage of plague victims may be a trick of the Black Police to capture you!"

Wentworth made no answer but went swiftly toward the car. There was scarcely room for him to walk between the police—every one of them was taller than his own six feet, and forming a flesh-and-blood shield between him and any assassins who might be lurking nearby. He was stepping into the sedan when a girl dodged past Kirkpatrick and ran toward the car. Kirkpatrick uttered a sharp cry and Wentworth whirled, hand leaping automatically to the gun beneath his armpit. He smiled then and let his hand drop. The girl caught his hands.

"There's no use in protesting, Dick!" she said swiftly. "I'm going with you! If there's any danger, my place is at your side. At least it can find us together!"

Wentworth looked down into her deep violet eyes, touched with gentle fingers the chestnut curls that softly framed her oval face. "No argument, Nita," he said gently, and handed her into the car. "Hurry, driver!" he called.

THE SEDAN lunged forward. The thin shriek of motorcycle sirens began and the thunder of their engines

was all about them. Ahead and to the rear, sedans full of armed men formed a convoy. Wentworth disliked it, but conceded in his tired brain that it was perhaps necessary. The last forty-eight hours had taught him that the allies of the criminals he had ousted were still viciously active—and they knew well their business of murder!

Nor were the threats to his life and the impending invasion of the hordes of the plague his only concern. The criminals he had driven from office had been legally elected, and this placed Wentworth in the position of seemingly leading an armed rebellion against duly constituted authorities! It did not matter that hundreds of citizens had been tortured and killed; that outrageous taxes had been collected by racketeering methods and pocketed by the criminals and their myrmidons, the Black Police; or that it was the state government that had released the plague on the populace. None of these things could be proved in courts....

"Dick—" Nita's voice was low—"have you been able to get any word about what Governor Whiting is going to do in Albany?"

Wentworth, relaxed against the cushions with the enforced inertia which alone enabled him to continue for long hours without rest, opened his gray-blue eyes slowly. "No word at all," he said quietly. "We know that the Black Police hold all the rest of the state. He may lead them against us. I hope so."

"You hope so, Dick! Oh, you mean that then you might be able to take over the entire state!"

Wentworth smiled. "What I'm afraid of, Nita, is that Governor Whiting will call on Washington to send federal troops against us. After all, we are… insurgents."

"But, Dick, you couldn't fight them!"

"No," Wentworth said slowly, "we *wouldn't* fight them." Wentworth was outside the law, but he had never turned his hand against the forces of the law, nor against any innocent person. As the Spider, that secret nemesis of all criminals, he had fought and killed criminals. Not even to save his own life, would he fight against federal troops. The state troops, the Black Police, were a different matter. They had been recruited from the underworld. Prison doors had been thrown open to flood their ranks. Not one of them but had been guilty of vile crimes under the crooked regime of Governor Whiting and the secret criminal power behind him whom Wentworth knew only by the name of the Master….

Wentworth sat more erectly and saw that the cars were rapidly nearing the outermost limits of the city. "You will stay in this car, Nita," he said crisply. "You'll be safer here, and I'll be safer since I can think only of myself."

Nita laughed, though there was tenderness in her eyes. "Dick, you never think of yourself!" she whispered.

Wentworth dropped his hand on hers, leaned forward to call to the driver. "Stop, and signal men from the other cars!" he ordered.

When the heavily armed men came toward him, Wentworth gave curt instructions in response to which his own car shot ahead of the others and they fell a hundred yards behind.

"Those poor devils with the plague trust me," he replied to

Nita's protests. "Shall I show that I don't trust them by driving up with an armed escort like some European dictator?"

HE WAS peering ahead now and, from the crest of a rise, he caught his first glimpse of the thousands who had marched on New York City in the hope of relief from their awful disease. They had been stopped here by the police and, like dirty flood waters, they swelled out over the fields on each side of the highway. They squatted on the ground in hopeless clusters—mothers with stricken children in their arms, listless aged men. But at the barricade the police had erected, there was another group. These were younger men and there was menace in their compact numbers. It was from them that the demand had come to see Wentworth. They had been lied to so much that their trust was worn thin. Yes, they had been promised help, but Wentworth....

Wentworth's lips set in a harsh line as the car rolled swiftly nearer and he saw more details of the horrors he had known he must find here. They believed in him, and by God, he would not fail them! It was for their sake that he had taken arms against the state government when he might so easily have fled to safety beyond its borders. It was for the sake of the people that he had so often risked his life as the Spider to fight their enemies....

"Stop here!" Wentworth ordered curtly, and punched open the door of the car.

"No, Dick!" Nita cried. "Let the car come closer, and...."

She stopped then, for already Wentworth was striding toward the close-packed group of men at the barricade. Resolutely, she drew an automatic from her handbag and held it ready in her hand, but her eyes were soft as she watched the steady swing of Wentworth's confident shoulders. They had borne so many burdens, but they never bowed even briefly in despair, such was the high courage of his heart. His head was high and there was no fatigue in the briskness of his stride, though he  had not slept in forty-eight hours and more… Nita masked the gun in her hand and stepped to the running-board of the car. Dear God, let nothing happen to him….

The police at the barricade snapped to salute at Wentworth's approach, but he only acknowledged that briefly and mounted the barrier at once.

"You sent for me," he called out to the assembled thousands. "Here I am!"

White faces turned up to him incredulously. In the forefront of the crowd, a woman stared, and Wentworth saw her throat jerk convulsively. She dropped to her knees and her hands were lifted as if she prayed.

"It's Richard Wentworth!" Her cry ran thinly through the chill air of early winter. "Richard Wentworth, our commander, has come!"

Voice after voice took up that cry until it rang to the arch of the heavens, and Wentworth felt the hot stinging tears in his eyes. He felt humble before such trust. And Kirkpatrick had been afraid of trickery! Men and women were pressing forward with their up-stretched, thin arms lifted to him. Wentworth lifted his hands.

"Please," he called. "Please, wait! Some medical supplies came with me and others will be sent as soon as possible. Also food.

Quarters will be cleared for you on the northern boundaries of the city as rapidly as possible! You will be taken care of. I only ask that you wait for a little while, a few hours more, until people can be cleared out of the northern district of the city. You don't want others to fall ill of this accursed plague. I know you'll wait!"

His eyes quested everywhere over the people. They had left the meager fires they had built for warmth and were huddled before him like sheep, like children, frightened of the dark. The ambulance loaded with medical supplies, which had accompanied him, rolled up to the barricade, and Wentworth turned to the police.

"Break down this barricade!" he ordered. "These people have promised to wait!"

IF THERE was any hesitancy in the police in obeying that order, it faded before Wentworth's stern eyes. The barricade was breached and the ambulance backed closer. Interns made ready their injections and Wentworth stepped down among the plague-stricken people. He took off his overcoat and put it around the shoulders of an old woman. Her hands, gripping it, were twisted with the torture of the plague and her lips were dumb.

Wentworth turned from her... and from the thick-pressed

RICHARD WENTWORTH

ranks of the mob a man stepped forward. He had one arm in a sling. He pointed the cast of his arm at Wentworth and, at point-blank range, fired a hidden gun straight at Wentworth's breast!

9

Wentworth saw the movement of the man's arm, and the trick was old enough for him to be suspicious of a gun hidden in the cast. And yet he was not. He was overwhelmed with the misery of these people and for once his ever-alert guard was down. Richard Wentworth would have died in that instant, except for one thing.

His kindness saved him. The old woman about whose shoulders he had placed his coat saw the movement and, with an inarticulate cry, she flung her body in the path of that bullet.

It tore cruelly into her worn back, and the impact of the brutal lead drove her into Wentworth's arms. He clasped her instinctively and fell with her to the ground. His hand belatedly leaped to his holstered gun. A moment before, there had been a thousand murmuring voices. Now they were stilled by the thunderclap of that shot. White faces stared in utter blank amazement at Wentworth, pitching to the ground with that aged woman clasped in his arms. But it endured only for a moment. Then a vast inchoate shout of rage lifted from a hundred throats. Before Wentworth could level his automatic and shoot down the assassin, a dozen men had thrown themselves between him and the killer!

Through the bedlam, Wentworth caught the angry shouts of the police; the hammer of engines as motorcycles and police cars raced forward. He sprang to his feet and, for a moment between the weaving heads of the crowd, he glimpsed the assassin. The man's face was bloodied and there were a score of fists beating at him. That much he saw before the assassin went down under the combined assault of an infuriated mob.

Wentworth sprang to the barricade and ordered the police back, then he leaped to the side of the old woman who had saved his life. He bent over her tenderly... and she was smiling. He bent close to her moving lips.

"My life," she whispered. "Nothing. You... you are the commander!"

Wentworth swung her into his arms and ran to the ambulance with her. "Quickly!" he rasped at the interns. "You must...."

He stopped then and something like a sob thrust hard and tearing into his throat. The old woman was already dead. Fury racked him. He sprang back to the barricade and flung a shout at the milling crowd beneath it. They could not hear him. He leaped down among them and fought his way to the midst of the brawling mob and finally they fell back... parted and let him gaze down on the thing that had been an assassin. He had been trampled into a shapeless mass upon the earth.

Wentworth's swift gaze brushed the faces of the men who stood around him. There was still fury in their eyes and horror. Wentworth said slowly, "It is well. I thank you. The relief work will proceed as rapidly as possible."

He turned heavily away and went back to the barricade and weariness weighted his heart. He had come to bring life—and death had followed him. It did not matter that this undoubtedly was an effort of the Black Police. To save him, that poor old woman... Nita was kneeling beside her, but it was futile. She rose as Wentworth came nearer and put her hand on his arm.

"Oh, Dick," she whispered. "I wanted to be with you!"

Wentworth shook his head. "I couldn't die with my work half

11

done, Nita," he said gently. It was a rededication of his life to the service he had chosen....

The loud racketing of a motorcycle engine, the scream of its siren, jerked Wentworth about swiftly toward the road, and a policeman courier leaped from a machine, running to Wentworth with a written message.

"From the commissioner!"

Wentworth ripped it open, and his lips drew into harsh lines. He knotted the message into a tight wad, gestured sharply to the police. "Carry on here. I'll rush more supplies." He turned and strode toward the barricades. "I'll have to reassure them," he said aside to Nita. "We have to leave at once!"

"The Black Police!" Nita cried.

"It's worse than that," Wentworth clipped out his words harshly. "Washington has ordered federal troops out against us. I have one hour to surrender the city—and all my men!"

CHAPTER 2
FLIGHT

BITTERNESS WAS in Wentworth's heart as he made his brief address to the plague victims, and rebellion sharpened his words. He had struck one shrewd blow at the Master who criminally ruled the state. From control of the city, his men might well move to an honest control of the entire state—and now in a single gesture the cup of success had been dashed from his lips. Oh, the Master played well!

There was one consolation. If the Master had found it necessary to appeal to federal troops against Wentworth and his men, it meant that his own control had been badly shaken. The Master would not want federal interference in the state… Wentworth sprang down from the barricade and raced back to his sedan, sent it speeding toward police headquarters.

An hour was none too much time, but he could count on Kirkpatrick to assemble their men for a speedy retreat. He would know that there was no other course open to them.

Already, army planes were circling overhead. They would not attack, of course, but at the first effort to escape from the city, they would give warning to headquarters….

As the sedan swept up to police headquarters, he saw the thick ranks of the men he had led to victory—barely a hundred of them left now. But they broke into cheers at sight of him, and Wentworth paused on the steps. A fierce resolve was forming in his mind.

"Men!" he called. "I have to lead you in retreat once more! But we will not lose everything we have gained here. The federal troops will take over New York City and it will be up to us to see that they stay here. I want a squad of volunteers to remain in the city and keep up an appearance of rebellion, stir the people to disorders—anything short of actual conflict with federal troops so that they will have an excuse to remain here. The probability is that you will be killed one by one…."

A sturdy man with a smiling, weathered face strode forward with the rolling stride of a seaman. "I'm your man, skipper," he touched his forelock. "We'll make them federals think there's a whole army hiding here."

Wentworth smiled in return. "Very well, Sailor Joe," he said quietly, but there was a choking in his throat. So many of his brave followers had died. Sailor Joe was almost the last of those who had first fled with him from New York City months ago when first the Master had shown his teeth.

"Ten men will do me, sir," Sailor Joe said and turned toward the bulk of the men. "Ten of you lubbers to die with Sailor Joe," he rasped out. "Stand forward!"

It was as if he had shouted, "Forward, march!" The entire company of men stepped forward, and Sailor Joe's deep laughter rolled out. He walked in front of the men and tallied them one by one to his side.

"The rest of you will have your chance at fighting," Wentworth assured them. "When we leave here, we march on Albany!"

He turned and strode into the headquarters with the eager shouts of the men ringing in his ears. Months of guerrilla warfare had made them wary and hard. And they would follow his lead into hell itself. With men such as these… Kirkpatrick rose grimly to his feet at Wentworth's entrance with Nita.

"I'm getting cars together for retreat," he said quietly. "Ready in ten minutes at the most." He knuckled the neatly waxed points of his mustache, a habit of his when he was worried. "I don't understand this demand for surrender without having made a demonstration in advance. You'd almost think they wanted us to escape."

"Either that or a trap!" Wentworth said quietly. "They may well throw out a force to the north of the city. A wise commander would prefer that to fighting through city streets."

Kirkpatrick's lips snapped together thinly. "That's it, then!" he said. "We'll send a police plane ahead. It can communicate with us by radio."

Wentworth shook his head again. "Not a chance. What makes me suspect a trap is the fact that there already are army planes overhead. They are there to prevent observation." He glanced at his watch. "Start the advance guard. We can move fast with our small force. Let the advance men take a two-way radio car."

Wentworth led the way presently to the same sedan in which he had raced to the barricades. The convoy waited, but he dismissed it curtly. "Federal troops will be here shortly. Until that time, it will be your business to hold this building and control of the police against the Black Police. They have no jurisdiction over you. If you'll phone the army headquarters on Governors' Island, I'm sure they'll authorize you for that."

One of the detectives, a gray-headed man with mild-seeming blue eyes, came forward and saluted. "We'd rather go with you, sir," he said. "There's plenty to hold headquarters."

Wentworth's smile was instant and warm, and he clapped a hand on the man's shoulder. "Sorry, MacGregor," he said quietly. "You forget that we are insurgents—rebels. If we're caught, we'll be lucky to escape execution before a firing squad. And you can serve better here. See that every possible evidence of Black Police crookedness is placed before the federal authorities."

WITHOUT FURTHER words then, Wentworth climbed

into the car and sent it racing toward the northern limits of the city. He was instantly relaxed against the cushions, conserving his energies for the action ahead. The need of sleep made a sick weight in his stomach, but his tired brain raced on with preparations for what lay ahead—trying to fathom federal plans and circumvent them. It was obvious that his best move would be to disband his men but he would not give up every hope of victory. If only they could reach Albany as a unit and smash the crooked government there when they were least expecting an attack….

That was it!

A shattering blast rocked the sedan, and Wentworth whipped erect in his seat to see a storm of earth settling a hundred yards to the right of the road where a bomb had been dropped. A second struck even nearer. The sedan swerved, then settled down to greater speed. The driver was hunched over the wheel. Wentworth's face was white, grimly set. They could make no answer to that attack….

"Smoke screen!" he snapped at the driver, saw the man's hand leap to a lever on the dashboard, and instants later black swirling smoke belched out behind the sedan. It made driving perilous, but at least it would mask the exact locations of the cars and make direct hits difficult.

The concussion of the bombs dropped behind, and Wentworth realized they were hammering through a small village. They would be safe here… safe only until troops could surround and smash them. That was the purpose of those planes overhead. Wentworth closed his lips thinly and did not speak. The sedan

whipped through the close cluster of
houses, and the bombing began again.

"Two cars hit," Kirkpatrick's voice
came out thick and harsh.

Wentworth's hands were white,
gripping his knees. This was complete

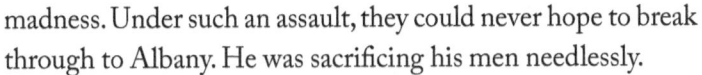

madness. Under such an assault, they could never hope to break
through to Albany. He was sacrificing his men needlessly.

Abruptly, an excited voice began to speak over the radio and,
from the weak signals, Wentworth recognized that it came
from the scout car ahead. "Road blocked by troops. Hundreds
of them. We're surrounded. We…" The man's voice broke in a
strangling gasp, and after that the radio's note sang on and on
without interruption except that the scattered thin repetition
of rifle shots came to their ears.

Wentworth's face was strained and white. "There's a consid-
erable woods ahead," he said, making his voice quiet only by
strong effort. "Turn off the road into them, driver, and sound
three long blasts, three shorts on your horn."

The signal bellowed out from the horn, and Wentworth heard
other automobile horns take it up behind him. An instant later,
the car lurched into the ditch, charged up a gentle slope and
lunged in among the trees.

"Disbandment?" Kirkpatrick asked quietly.

Wentworth lifted his shoulders heavily. "There's nothing else.
I can't have all the men killed. We can't defend ourselves."

Other cars were slamming into the woods and the men
climbed out rapidly, began to form up under the low, swift orders

of under officers. Abruptly, Wentworth bent close to the radio. There was a whisper coming from it, a faint whisper....

"Black Police," the whisper came. "Looting town. Hundreds of them. Three companies are..." There was a thunderous blast of a shot, and the radio went dead.

Kirkpatrick and Wentworth stared at each other. Here was a faint hope. If it was only the Black Police who blocked their path, then the men could fight. And looting a town! That was a call the Spider could not ignore; his men would not... He strode rapidly toward them.

"Men," he began abruptly. "Our way is blocked by Black Police who are looting the town of Westphalian. The bombers are apparently army men. We can disband here and most of us win through, or we can attack..." He got no farther, for the voices of the men were drowning him out, and there was no mistaking the tenor of their shouts: *"Lead us!"* they shouted. *"Lead us! Attack!"*

Wentworth lifted his hands. "I expected no less," he said quietly. "If we can smash through the Black Police, we will rendezvous in Westphalian. After that, I hope to push on to Albany. It will be a fight to the finish there. All our camps are destroyed... but victory may be within our reach if we can strike. Here is our battle plan...."

SWIFTLY, WENTWORTH outlined it. He had no need to consult a map for he knew the territory perfectly. Two cars would dash along the road they had been following, until they established contact with the Black Police. Then they would retreat and attempt to draw the police with them.

The remaining eight cars would divide evenly and advance along parallel roads to attack the flanks.

"The idea is not to destroy the Black Police, but to reach Westphalian!" he finished. "If the people are being attacked there, we can count on recruiting more forces to wipe out the Black Police."

He swung back to the leading sedan and rapidly examined the motorcycle which was carried on a special rack behind it, found it in working order.

"The plan's good," Kirkpatrick said somberly. "It would be better if some one could reach the town and organize a sortie...."

Wentworth smiled, nodded, as he swung the motorcycle to the ground. "That's my job," he said. "No, Kirk, it's the barricades all over again. They'll follow... *the Spider!*"

As he spoke, he unlocked the trunk behind the sedan and took out a mirror, a shallow make-up tray and set to work on his face. "The Spider must be dead," he said quietly. "I can't see why else he would have remained idle during this fight with the Master. Since he has not shown himself, I'll have to substitute again...."

Kirkpatrick's face held its stiff, unyielding lines. He had long been convinced that Wentworth and the Spider were one, though he had never found the proof of that closely held secret. As police commissioner of New York City, it had been his duty—and he was not a man to swerve from duty at any cost—to track down the Spider because, in legal eyes, the Spider's executions of criminals could be regarded only as murder. It was for Kirkpatrick's sake—and in the hope that he would one day resume his post as commissioner—that Wentworth hid his double identity behind the subterfuge of "posing" as the Spider.

"Why not abandon this pretense, Dick?" Kirkpatrick demanded abruptly. "If your men know that you actually were the Spider, instead of merely pretending to be, their morale would be stronger."

Wentworth smiled and nodded toward the men. Standing loosely in formation, they were singing a marching song together, their faces bright, eager, dedicated. "Their morale couldn't be stronger," Wentworth said. "As to this masquerading as the Spider, I don't like it, but the people of Westphalian will need a more colorful leader than Richard Wentworth behind whom to rally. I only wish the Spider were active."

There was a touch of bitterness in Wentworth's voice as he rapidly daubed his face with a liquid that sallowed the skin and drew it tautly over the cheekbones. He blamed himself endlessly for his failures actually to identify and kill the Master. Twice he had trapped the man in clever disguises and each time* the man had managed to elude the Spider's swift justice. Now again the Master had disappeared into obscurity and, until he could be found out and destroyed, Wentworth knew that all

---

* AUTHOR'S NOTE: The details of Wentworth's previous battles with the Master and the latter's almost miraculous escapes from the Spider are told in the two previous issues of the Spider's adventures and are entitled "The City That Paid to Die" and "The Spider at Bay."

his maneuvers against the Black Police must be merely temporary measures—a treatment of symptoms and their alleviation, instead of a cure for the disease that was destroying the state he loved.

And yet he could not abandon the people he served to the tyrannies and tortures of the Black Police. It was a fact that the Master had struck so often and so rapidly that it had taken all Wentworth's skill to contrive adequate defense of himself and his forces. There had been little time to track down the murderous Master.

Wentworth's hands rapidly fashioned his nose into a hawk-like predatory beak but the lipless gash they made of his mouth could not have been more grim than his thoughts. Once more the Master had him on the run; once more the man was hiding behind the swift and deadly progress of events. The man was a phantom—but none the less deadly.

Swiftly Wentworth finished the disguise of the Spider—bushy black brows over his own, a lank long wig. The face he had created was sinister, and it had carried terror to many a criminal. He drew on a black slouch hat, and swung a long cape from his shoulders. The cape was no longer the black, somber thing of other days when he had needed to have it merge with the background of furtive shadows. It was brilliant green.

"For visibility!" he explained with a short laugh. "I want people to notice me now!"

"But Dick," it was Nita at his side. "It makes you a—a perfect target! At least a bullet-proof vest...."

"Too heavy," Wentworth said curtly. "I'm off, Kirk. You know my plan. Give me ten minutes before you start the cars down the main road. By that time, you should be able to have your flanking cars in position, too. See you in Westphalian!"

He sprang to the saddle of the motorcycle and Nita clung to him, but only for a moment. She stepped bravely back then. Their lives were made up of such partings and well each of them knew that they might never meet again in this world. Nita's hands were small, white fists at her sides.

"See you in Westphalian!" she cried gaily, and, while Wentworth could see her, she held her brave smile. But when his motorcycle had jounced out of sight on the race through the woods, tears were on her cheeks as she turned to Kirkpatrick.

"What's my job, Stanley?" she asked quietly then.

Kirkpatrick's frosty blue eyes rested kindly on her. "I need a machine-gunner in my car," he said. He glanced at his watch, waiting. Off to the northward, a bomb burst, and fragments clattered through the stripped limbs of the trees. A huge oak lifted bodily and climbed up thirty, forty feet into the air before it toppled and came crashing back.

Kirkpatrick waved a signal, and eight of the cars began to work their way off toward the parallel roads. It was characteristic of Kirkpatrick that he chose the most dangerous post for himself—in the two cars that were to draw the fire of the Black Police. He was very dapper, very straight as he stood, eyes returning now and again to his watch. There was, as always, a gardenia in his lapel....

Abruptly, he moved toward his car, climbed into the front

beside the driver. "All ready, Frank," he said quietly. *On to West-phalian!*"

THROUGH THE narrow lanes of the woods, Wentworth wheeled the motorcycle rapidly. The green cape billowed out from his shoulders like some knight's surplice. No knight ever had a more devoted sense of service than Wentworth, but there was nothing bright or eager about his grim-lined face. Battle lay ahead, and the risk of sudden death. Not that Wentworth feared death. They had been familiars on too many perilous expeditions, but he respected that universal antagonist—and Wentworth must not die… yet. He could not leave his task unfinished.

Thoughts of death rode coldly with him now. There was an icy bite to the wind that was not all the breath of December, and it irritated him. His eyes roved ceaselessly ahead, picking out the likeliest path for his race—watching, too, for ambush. The burst of a searching bomb thrust at him, and the concussion sucked at his clothing. Death… but it must not find him in any petty skirmish in the woods. It must not strike while the Master still lived and dominated all the state, twisting it into a private domain for his pilfering.

Wentworth burst from the cover of the woods and began a swift race across the fields. There were a half dozen planes in the air and, even as he spotted them, one wheeled in a swift bank and began a fierce swoop toward him. Wentworth had to school himself to caution. Fatigue was a perpetual goad to recklessness and he was feeling the drain of all those sleepless hours. He raced on—and checked between low stone walls that wandered along a farm lane.

It was the beginning of the end. Panic shook them—some
even abandoned their guns as they took to their heels!

He heard presently the splatting fury of machine-gun bullets
shattered on the rocks; heard the angry snarl of malformed
lead. A small bomb burst so close that his senses reeled, but the
stone wall stood him in good stead. Presently, the plane had

swooped on to other prey and he once more, reelingly, mounted his motorcycle to speed on.

Moments later, he crossed the parallel road to which he had assigned four of the automobiles, but he pushed on. The Black Police patrols would have this covered and he must reach the town without interception. He must expect to find sentries, at least… His thoughts flew back to Nita, to Kirkpatrick, and he glanced at his watch. Ten minutes only had passed. They would

be starting now on their dash down the central road. A renewed blasting of bombs told him grimly that the cars had left the cover of the woods. The battle was in the hands of the gods now—or in his own. He must hasten to the town and rouse the townspeople to a sortie that would smash the power of the police.

Hours seemed to dribble past while he wheeled the motorcycle at a terrific pace along the concrete road into which he had turned. Rifle fire came dimly to his ears through the hiss and hammer of the wind; through the flapping fury of his trailing cape. He wrenched the throttle open to the last notch, laid the machine far over on a curve—and spotted a picket of Black Police dead ahead! Three men were crouched in a covert of heaped-up brush—motorcycle and side-car mounted a machine gun. Even as Wentworth spotted them, they opened fire!

Only Wentworth's terrific speed saved him in that first instant. They had waited until they sighted him to open fire and in that brief heartbeat of time, his machine had covered many feet. Wentworth whipped one hand to an automatic beneath his armpit and emptied it in a swift drum roll of fire, as he swept past the machine gun. The men were struggling to wheel it about, to bring its sights to bear on Wentworth. High accuracy was impossible even for the Spider's unerring guns, but he saw one man hammered limply back across the gun; heard the hissing blast of a motorcycle tire let go. Then Wentworth was past and drilling on toward the city.

A belated blast of bullets hurricaned after him, but too late. The next instant, Wentworth swooped around another curve—and the town of Westphalian spread out below him.

UNDER THE gray arch of the skies, it was neat and pleasant—homes set among trees that, though barren now, still held the grace of spring promise, a few parallel business streets were in its center. But Wentworth guessed at what loot the Black Police aimed. There was a powerful bank here and wealthy. They could sack that and lay the blame on "rebellion"... One long thoroughfare stretched out before Wentworth and he saw that it was blocked by barricades. Then he swooped down another hill and all the town was blotted out. Something wet spattered against his face and he was conscious of whirling black specks... It was snowing.

Wentworth felt a great lifting of his heart. If only the snow would thicken! It would blot out visibility from the skies above, render the planes useless. If it continued, his men might still escape! He skated the motorcycle around a corner and into the first street of Westphalian—then a shout of anger leaped to his lips. The Black Police were being very thorough about their siege. It was their barricade Wentworth had spotted from above and it dosed the street against escape from within. But the Black Police had not been content with barricading. There were upright posts atop the chest-high barrier, and to each post a woman had been bound!

One of the Black Police turned about leisurely at the sound of his motor. They were not expecting enemies from without! When he saw Wentworth, he stared for an incredulous moment before he could voice an alarm. Wentworth whipped his machine in between two buildings and was instantly on the ground. With steady, furious fingers he loaded the emptied automatic and then, with a gun in each hand, he moved steadily toward the corner of the building.

There were a half dozen of the Black Police at the barricade. Others might be quartered in near-by houses. He would have to risk that. After all, he had fourteen bullets, and the range was less than fifty yards. The Spider's almost miraculous aim was equal to greater distances and long years had taught him the perfection of his test-barreled firearms. He stepped deliberately into the open. Three police were huddled together with the man who first had spotted him. So swift had been Wentworth's return that they had not yet decided on their course of action. Wentworth opened fire....

With the steadiness of a man on target-range, Wentworth's two guns rose and fell alternately. Three blasts, and those three men were down. One of the remaining three managed to get his rifle to his shoulder, but he was flustered and frightened. Brief seconds after the green-caped Spider stepped out from the shelter of the house, he was reloading his guns—and the Black Police were dead.

He walked swiftly forward. The women, bound to the posts, were straining white faces about toward him, but as yet he did not speak to them. He paused beside one of the dead police and, deliberately, pressed the base of a thin cigarette lighter to the man's forehead. When he straightened, there was a glowing crimson mark on the whitening dead flesh, a thing of sprawling hairy legs and poison fangs—*the seal of the Spider!*

Not until then did Wentworth face the women, and he saw

tears of thanksgiving in their eyes. A girl, between joyous laughter and tears, lifted her face to the heavens.

"Thank God!" she cried. "Oh, thank God. Now we are saved! The Spider has come!"

Wentworth leaped to the barricade beside her and used a pocket knife on her bonds. For a moment, she shrank from him, for his face was the sinister countenance of the Spider. Then, as he finished freeing her, their eyes met and, swiftly, the girl smiled. She tossed the thick black hair that framed her face and laughed at him.

"If your enemies could see your eyes as I see them now," she said softly. "They would never fear you again! You are... *good!*"

Wentworth's gaze took in the firm strong line of her jaw and the determination in her mouth and nodded. He needed her help now.

"Take this knife," he ordered swiftly, "and cut all these other women free. Get everyone of them to a telephone and tell them to call numbers at random through the phone book. Tell the people the Spider has come to save them. His men are on the march. The people must meet me in the center of Westphalian. Pershing Square? Good! They are to bring every weapon they can lay their hands on! We'll destroy the Black Police!"

WENTWORTH RACED back to his motorcycle and, when he wheeled it into the street, all the women had disappeared save the black-haired girl. She was waiting calmly beside the barricade with a rifle slung across her shoulder and another, bayonet fixed, in her hands.

"Let the others do women's work," she said pleadingly to

Wentworth, "I can use a rifle like a man. You'll need every good shot you can get!"

Wentworth smiled in spite of himself. If he could only gain a following of such brave souls, they would wipe out the Black Police this day! Her words were the sort Nita would have uttered… Wentworth's heart went cold for a moment, realizing the danger into which Nita must be moving with his men. He must hurry!

"On behind," he snapped at the girl.

She sprang immediately to the rear fender of the motorcycle and he began a swift ride through the city streets, shouting as he went—shouting the news that the Spider had come to save them. Windows were flung wide, and white faces peered after him. The girl added her shouts to his.…

"Must we women do your fighting for you?" she demanded scornfully. She brandished the rifle aloft at the white faces.

Men began to stream into the streets, and their shouts added to the din, drew others to the defense of their homes. They were brave enough. They needed only a leader and, God being willing, Wentworth would lead them! A mob of men followed him at a dead run toward Pershing Square. They brandished rifles and shotguns, revolvers, clubs. The battened door of a butcher shop flung open and the butcher, still in his white, stained apron, dashed out into the street waving a long knife and a cleaver. Wentworth heard his bellow above many others. "Kill the Black Police! Kill them!" The air was suddenly alive with the clatter of gunshots that echoed in all directions as men, gathering their courage, attacked the barricades of the Black Police. Women were joining the march now, armed ludicrously with brooms, rolling pins. But it was their courage that counted, and the example they set their men. Ahead of him, Wentworth saw a woman with a baby in her arms. She ran into the middle of the street and stood almost in his path.

As he rolled past, he heard the woman speak to her child, "Look, Junior. Look, and don't forget this ever! You have seen him! The Spider! The greatest man…."

Wentworth felt his heart swell within him and his fatigue and despair were forgotten. How could any man fail when people would follow him like this! This single thing was worth all the years or risking death, of battling against hopeless odds. His lips tightened with resolution. No matter how futile the battle seemed, he would never stop until the Master was destroyed, or death… Wentworth did not complete the thought. He would defy even death to stop him!

The girl whispered in his ear, "We'll win! Oh, I know we'll win. Pershing Square is just ahead. See the people. Thousands of them! But… if trouble comes! If you're hurt, come to the home of Maria Laplante! You'll be safe there!"

Wentworth said gently, "Thank you, Maria." He was to remember that….

Wentworth wheeled the motorcycle into Pershing Square and men already were jamming into it from every side. Wentworth sprang to the pedestal of Pershing's statue which stood in its midst and held up his arms for attention. He looked slowly over the white intent faces about him. The snow was falling with a slow dignity now, great white flakes that were gentle as a benediction. It clung to his hands before the warmth of his body melted it. And the sky was darkening, the menace of the planes gone....

"My men are already attacking the Black Police at three points to the south," he called clearly. "Will you let me lead you out to destroy the Black Police before it's too late?"

The shout that answered him rang up to the heavens, and a slow smile spread over Wentworth's grim-shaped lips. These men might know little of warfare, but they would be avenging a thousand indignities and crimes. They needed only a leader, and God willing....

"Southward then!" Wentworth shouted and pointed to the main road. "We will divide their forces in half, roll them up on themselves and... *destroy them!*"

"Destroy them!" the men echoed.

Wentworth leaped to the ground and back to his motorcycle. He rolled it through the thick press of the men, and they opened an aisle for him. On every side, he saw whitely determined faces, heard their pledges and beheld the idolatry of their eyes as they rested on the green-caped figure of the Spider. Impossible to make any plan for battle; but equally impossible to envisage failure so long as he could lead these men!

BEFORE WENTWORTH reached the first barricade, men had swept the Black Police from the spot. More and more fighters were joining the ranks every moment. The hammering of heavy rifles reached Wentworth's ears now, coming from east and west. His men had joined battle and the Black Police before him were disconcerted. They could not know the strength of the forces behind them. For a few minutes, they maintained their fire, and around Wentworth men fell—but there was no faltering in the advance.

A half dozen of the Black Police jumped up from their hideouts and began to run. It was the beginning of the end. Panic shook them. Some even abandoned guns as they took to their heels. The citizens of Westphalian were everywhere. Guns blasted and, when there were no guns, the men raced eagerly ahead with clubs and brandished knives. Those Black Police who fell into their hands did not long survive—and each death brought a new weapon to the defenders of the city.

The charge had become a slaughter. Here and there the Black Police attempted a stand, but were quickly wiped out. They were criminals and did not have the courage to stand in open battle. Theirs was the bravery that preyed on helpless people, but against such headlong, reckless morale as the citizens showed, they were terrified.

Finally, Wentworth called a halt and started the men back toward Westphalian. Dusk was beginning to fall and there was a wind that whirled the snow about him in eddying gusts. Already, some of the dead were beginning to find their shrouds of white. The victory had been won, but there was a tight, worried frown on Wentworth's forehead.

Though they had advanced ten miles from the city limits, and the road was entirely cleared, he had found no trace of the two cars which were to have pushed down that central way—the path that he knew Kirkpatrick and Nita would have chosen for their own. He hurried the return, racing for Pershing Square which was to be the rendezvous, too, of his men.

He sighted from afar the half dozen cars that stood there. Windows were shattered from them and a crude dressing-station had been set up to care for the wounded. Wentworth raced ahead of the citizens on his motorcycle and flung his anxious inquiries at the men. There was no word of Nita or Kirkpatrick. All these had left Kirkpatrick in the wood and since then there had been nothing. Yes, there had been heavy firing on the central road, and several bombs....

Wentworth's face tautened at the news. Nita had warned him that his green cape would make him a target, but he had ridden unscathed through a pitched battle, and she....

The rifle shot was not loud against the low whine of the mounting wind, and the bullet did not cause much pain, at first. It struck Wentworth somewhere in the back, he knew. The shock drove him forward to his knees. He was aware of his men's angry shouts, of them crowding about to shield him with their own bodies, from the assassins. Then he felt only a spreading numbness that seemed to reach to his very soul, and the grateful cool of the thin snow against his cheek.

He tried to arouse himself, to order the men to seek their own safety. Federal troops would press hard on their trail, he knew, and the Black Police would return in force. Without a leader, the citizens would be helpless again. He tried... but no sound came from his lips. His twilight faded almost instantly into night....

SOMETIME THAT first night, Wentworth recovered consciousness briefly and found himself in a low-roofed cellar with many of his men about him. The bullet had pierced his lung, a grave-faced doctor told him. It was a critical wound. He might live....

Wentworth's lips pulled back from his teeth with the effort the smile cost him. "I will live," he said faintly. "I still have work to do. I want my men here. All of them. At once!"

The doctor's clean-shaven cheeks drew in with gravity. "I can't allow it," he said sharply. "Any excitement... Didn't you understand me? The wound is very serious!"

Wentworth tried to push himself up on his elbows, but the effort was too much for him and a tearing cough brought the taste of blood to his lips. He lay quiet for a moment. "My men, doctor. All of them, and at once!"

From the shadows, a dark, bearded man with a white turban on his head stepped forward. His hand was on the hilt of a knife at his belt. "My master ordered his men!" he said sharply.

Relief flooded Wentworth's heart. This was his own trusty servitor, Ram Singh, who had been with one of the flanking actions. With him here to enforce his orders... Wentworth closed his eyes and rested. He heard movement around him and knew that the men were assembling. There was a weight about his heart and breathing was a painful, draining effort. Presently, a hand touched Wentworth's arm and he opened his eyes to the concerned worshiping eyes of Ram Singh. Wentworth smiled faintly.

"I won't die, Ram Singh," he whispered. "I have work to do. Repeat my words to the men... These are orders. They are to hide their weapons, disperse, scatter at once over the state. When I can lead them again, I will recall them."

Ram Singh repeated the orders and sharp protests arose from the men. When presently, Wentworth whispered again, there was the silence of death in the low-ceilinged room.

"Federal troops are close," Wentworth said. "Black Police are coming, bent on revenge. I'm safe here. You would be sure to be found—and hanged! All our leaders are gone, Kirkpatrick, Miss van Sloan…" Pain stopped him then, and he could not guess whether it was the pain of the bullet, or of his own words. "You are thinking of me when you want to stay here. I know that. But so many of you hiding here will be more easily found than I would, hiding alone. And there are not enough of us to resist a big force. You must go. At once! When I am well and the time is ripe, I'll call you together again…" A tearing cough broke in on his straining words, and Ram Singh's strong, nasal voice caught up his mandates and thundered them out.

A girl's voice joined with the Sikh's insistently and, for a wild hopeful moment, Wentworth thought that it was Nita… He forced himself up on his elbow. No, it was the black-haired girl of the barricades, Maria Laplante. Wentworth felt his senses slipping from him. He was bleeding again….

Apparently, Ram Singh had dominated. The men were filing past him one by one in leave-taking and there were tears on their faces. Wentworth's own eyes stung. God knew whether he would ever see these brave ones again, see Kirkpatrick and… and Nita. He tried to reassure the men, but the room whirled before him. His eyes grew dim. A caught… His senses blacked out.

CHAPTER 3
THE SPIDER IS DEAD!

NITA VAN SLOAN had recognized at the beginning of Kirkpatrick's foray against the middle of the Black Police lines before Westphalian, that he had chosen the most dangerous post for himself. But even then she was not prepared for the fury of the attack which immediately manifested itself. Two machine guns concentrated their fire on the two cars, in which Kirkpatrick's small group moved forward, and wiped it out.

Somehow, Nita managed to grip the wheel of the car and wrench it from the road, send it crashing over among the trees. It was not until the thickness of the growth had cut off the storm of bullets that she realized she was alone in the car. The others were all dead and Kirkpatrick… She bent swiftly over him and found that he, at least, was still alive. The bullet had ploughed through his shoulder and driven him to the floor. Even as she examined the wound, he was stirring, forcing himself up.

She urged him to his feet, and, half-carrying him, led Kirkpatrick out into the winter-barren woods. Fortunately, the snow began to fall soon afterward and the darkening of the sky threw black shadows in the woods. It was during this breathing space that Nita found a thick clump of hemlock and, in its protection, bound up Kirkpatrick's shoulder. Afterward, they crouched in the thicket, guns in hand, and listened to the crescendo of gunfire, now near at hand and again thin with distance. Gradually, the tone of the trepidation changed, became steady and drew closer.

Nita drew in a slow breath and let it out again. It seemed to her that she had been holding her breath for hours. "Dick got the townspeople together," she said slowly. "He's driving the police back!"

Kirkpatrick's grim lips relaxed in a slight smile. "Did you ever doubt that he would? I can't think of Dick and failure at the same time. Just as I can never imagine death stopping him. It seems to me that Dick will live forever, ageless, fighting the people's battles. Sometimes..." He hesitated.

Kirkpatrick was not a demonstrative, nor an especially imaginative man, but there was a quiver of emotion in his voice as he went on. "Sometimes, I think that Dick must be the embodiment of all those ancient heroes—the saviors of mankind. Only they died, and Dick lives on and on"

"Don't!" Nita cried. "Oh, don't! I... I'm superstitious." She laughed a little after she had said it, but her eyes were dark with fear.

A crashing in the underbrush jerked her suddenly tense and she peered out, gun ready. Three of the Black Police were dashing through the woods but Nita saw at once that she and Kirkpatrick were in no danger from them. They ran wildly, without weapons, their faces white with terror. Truly, Dick had won his battle! It was long hours afterward that she and Kirkpatrick made their way into Westphalian and learned that Wentworth had been shot down in his moment of victory, but she could find no trace of him. The townspeople either were too suspicious to talk, or they honestly did not know where the Spider had been carried.

"His men took him away," a man told her in a whisper. "I don't know where. But if you're friends of his, you'd better get out of town. The Black Police..." The man peered  over his shoulder and suddenly took to his heels.

Nita stared where the man had glanced and saw a squad of Black Police marching grimly through the streets and, in their wake, rolled armored cars of the U.S. Army! Federal troops were taking over the city, and Nita knew that, as the ally of an armed rebel, she could expect no help there! She bundled Kirkpatrick into a hastily commandeered car and raced away toward the hill country to the northward. She escaped, but her heart was heavy within her. Dick wounded... and a fugitive from the combined forces of the army and the Black Police!

THE DAYS that followed were frantic with worry. The radio carried notices of huge rewards for the capture of any rebel, and troops scoured the hill country. More than once, she and Kirkpatrick barely escaped them. It was a week after the disastrous victory at Westphalian that the radio brought Nita the news that turned her into a grief-stricken automaton.

She and Kirkpatrick were driving steadily northward over roads that were no more than rutted lanes over the mountains, picking a slow and perilous way by night, for they dared not move by day. The radio brought them news of a constantly widening search, of the capture of many of their allies, and then finally....

"Flash!" cried the announcer. "Here is the biggest news of

the day and it means the rebellion is permanently crushed. The Spider is dead! His body, still attired in the green cape he wore when last seen in Westphalian, was brought into Albany today. It was riddled with bullets...."

Nita uttered a choked cry and covered her face with her hands, and Kirkpatrick wrenched the car to a halt on the verge of a cliff that would have meant death to them both. His face was dead white in the back-glow of light from the dashboard and his mouth was knife-thin. He did not turn off the radio.

"The Spider," the radio announcer rushed on, "was tracked to earth in a cellar in Westphalian where he had hidden, wounded, ever since the armed rebellion he stirred up in that city was crushed. In the face of overwhelming odds, he tried to shoot it out with the Black Police who found him, but this time there were too many for him. He was literally shot to pieces."

Nita whispered, "I can't stand any more, Stanley. I...."

Kirkpatrick's hand trembled as he shut off the radio. "It isn't necessarily true," he said, dull-voiced, but his apathy destroyed the optimistic tenor of his words. "The Black Police might put out a message like that to stop all resistance. It might be that the federal troops are in their way here in the state. In fact, we know they are. They keep the Master from going on with his looting. If Washington thought the Spider was dead, they would call off the troops...."

Nita's head came up slowly. "You don't believe any of that, Stanley," she said. "It sounded too—*true*...."

"The Master is clever, Nita."

"Yes," Nita whispered. "Yes—clever. I won't believe it, Stanley. Because I can't let myself! Stanley, we'll have to… keep on fighting, alone now. If the Master has killed Dick…" Her voice broke and strangling sobs shook her whole body.

Kirkpatrick sat by helplessly. There was so little anybody could do at a time like this. Finally, he persuaded Nita to let him drive and began to push on deeper into the hills. Dick Wentworth… *dead.*

It was hours before Nita's high courage lifted her from the utter despondency into which she had fallen.

"Stanley," she said, "I'm going to Albany!"

"It's certain capture, Nita!" Kirkpatrick protested. "What can you accomplish?"

Nita shook her head. "Perhaps nothing, but I'm going. Perhaps, I can make sure whether Dick is really dead. Regardless, I'm going to get together what men of ours are left alive and go on with the fight! Don't forget, Ram Singh was with us. He has not been reported dead. Somehow, he would have found his way to Dick, and…" She drew in a deep breath. "I'm going to Albany, to find the Master, and destroy him!"

"That's madness!" Kirkpatrick knew he was arguing in vain.

Nita got a small smile on her lips. "I'm going to Albany!" she said softly.

Kirkpatrick was silent but, when the road forked presently, he turned the car back toward Albany. Perhaps, when Nita was convinced of her plan's futility, he could persuade her to leave the state. Afterward… but God alone knew if there would be any "afterward" with which to concern himself! His frosty blue eyes were gentle as they rested on Nita.

Into the doorway, a sub-machine gun in
his hands, stepped the Spider!

NITA COULD find out nothing about the body identified as the Spider, when she reached Albany. It had been secretly buried, and even from that she garnered hope though she knew it was equally logical that the burial would be kept secret to prevent any disorders at the funeral.

She began to make her plans. Plainly, the best idea was for her to get stenographer work in some state office while Kirk-

patrick traveled quietly over the state and assembled whatever men of theirs still were left alive. He would know at least where to find Jackson, Wentworth's chauffeur, who had been his sergeant during the war, the energetic and cheerful Sailor Joe, and perhaps Samuel Rice, the colonel of national guard who had thrown in his lot with Wentworth.

With that force as a nucleus; something might be accomplished. Kirkpatrick fell in with her plans reluctantly. His hesitancy was not from fear, but out of sheer hopelessness of success. Since Wentworth had failed despite all his knowledge of such battles, what could they hope to accomplish? However, he yielded to Nita and started out to assemble the men.

In the lodging she had obtained, Nita attempted a slight disguise. She had learned the art under a master, Richard Wentworth, and she applied herself diligently. She straightened her crisp curls and donned glasses; masked her figure somewhat in misfit clothing. And she abandoned the usual erect, self-confident carriage of shoulders and head. Wentworth's precept was that a person was more often identified by manner of walking than by facial appearance… Apparently, her plan succeeded. In a surprisingly few days, she had landed a position, not only with the government, but in the outer office itself of the lieutenant-governor, Marvin Rixson!

Nita took this for an augury of success for her plans and drove herself strenuously forward in her self-appointed task of learning the plans of the Black Police, who were Rixson's especial charge. What she learned there drove her close to despair. The Black Police had completely reestablished their dominion, not only in New York City where Wentworth had so recently triumphed, but throughout the state. Since the invasion of federal troops and their withdrawal—since news of the Spider's death had been broadcast, no one dared to resist their edicts. To be sure, a man now and then flew in the face of certain death to home or loved ones, but such outbreaks were sporadic, without plan—and utterly futile. Those who defied the Black Police merely died.

It was in her second week in the office that Nita began to get some inkling of the Master's plans. She copied over a series of orders for concentrations of the Black Police about three key cities in the state. What action would be taken against them, she did not know—but she could guess! When the black vultures, who wore the garb of the police, foregathered, there was looting and torture ahead! She would make sure that warnings were sent. This was the day Kirkpatrick had said he would return. Perhaps, they could work out some process for ferreting out the Master. Surely, in the presence of such a major operation, he would be somewhere near the center of action....

The winter night had fallen when Nita made her way out of the state office building and hurried toward the poor lodging she had taken. Even this early, the patrols of the Black Police were active, and five times before she reached her lodging she was stopped and ordered to show her papers. God, how could they hope to fight against such an organization as this! Nita's full lips tightened. If only Kirkpatrick had returned....

She hurried to her room, switched on her lights and her eyes flew to her mirror. There was a bit of red ribbon tied to the right side and, and, seeing that, Nita smiled for the first time in days. It meant that Kirkpatrick was back and would wait for her at the rendezvous! Nita had to force herself to eat and then once more she braved the police patrols. They seemed thicker tonight than ever before and a cold apprehension touched Nita's heart. What if her identity had been known all along, and she was being used to trap the rest of Wentworth's brave followers!

Nita fought down her fears and hurried on toward the meeting place they had fixed before Kirkpatrick's departure—the lobby of a motion picture theater. Three times she doubled on her trail, but she could find no evidence that she had been followed. Time and again she had to present her credentials to patrols of police. Finally, she entered the theater lobby and saw Kirkpatrick's lean form unfold itself from a chair. He looked shabby and was trying hard to hide the military erectness of his shoulders. He walked with a slight limp. There was no mistaking the gladness in his eyes.

"Maybe our luck has turned a little," he said softly. "You're safe—and I have found three men."

Nita's heart sank at the smallness of the results, but she kept her brave smile. "Good!" she whispered. "I have work for them." **THEY SAID** no more during the hour they thought it necessary to remain in the theater. When they went out, Black Police were outside, examining the papers of every person who emerged at the exit.

"I have credentials," Kirkpatrick whispered.

They went past that obstacle without difficulty, but it seemed to Nita that the sergeant in charge peered harder at them than at the others. She said nothing until Kirkpatrick handed her into a taxi.

"I'm frightened," she whispered then. "I've never seen so many patrols, and did you see how that sergeant stared at us?"

"Imagination," Kirkpatrick assured her.

However, Nita saw that he glanced now and again at their back trail and, after they left the taxi, he moved circuitously toward the garage where he told her he had stationed the men.

"Jackson is with me," he said. "Colonel Rice, Sailor Joe. That's all. So many of our men have been captured."

"And there's still no trace of Ram Singh?"

"None, Nita. But that's a hopeful sign, if anything can be hopeful."

Nita made no answer and tried to drive her mind to some plans for using the small force they had. Instead, her thoughts persistently returned to the prevalence of the Black Police. She put a smile on her lips as Kirkpatrick led her through an echoing, black garage, up a ramp and to a small, windowless room on the third floor. In response to Kirkpatrick's signal, the door opened cautiously and then she was ushered rapidly inside.

A single dim candle burned on a rough table. There were a few chairs—nothing more in the room—and three men. They crowded around her and, at the sight of their familiar faces, Nita felt tears sting her eyes. She held out both her hands to the bluff Colonel Rice, to the still cheerful Sailor Joe and Jackson. Jackson's face was gaunt and the knotted muscles of his jaw, always prominent, seemed to have swollen his cheeks. His eyes were bleak.

"I'm not good for much, Miss Nita, but to take orders," he said flatly. "But I can promise you this. You point out the men who died for Major Wentworth and I... I'll do the rest!" His hands closed into white-hard knots.

Nita touched his fist with her own hand. "Well do it together, Jackson," she promised. She swung to the others. "None of you, then, has heard anything from Dick? Nothing that would indicate he was still alive?"

The silence of the men was answer enough. Nita had not known until that moment how much she had hoped... She shook her head to clear it of grief. Only in action could there be any relief. She swiftly began to outline what she had learned of the concentration of men about the three cities.

"Almost certainly, that means looting or action against some groups of people in those cities," she went on. "With our reduced force, we can only hope to warn them. What I want to devise is some means of forcing the Master out into the open, and then...."

Jackson's tense white face filled out her sentence. He, more than any of them save Nita, had built his life about Wentworth.

Kirkpatrick said slowly, "I once masqueraded as the Spider. I can do it again. Perhaps, if the Master thought the Spider was still alive...."

There was no warning of the attack. It came with the suddenness of a gunshot from the dark. The door slammed open and the opening was jammed with the Black Police, guns in hand, eyes alert and hard!

The voice that commanded surrender came from behind them

and, as the Black Police pushed in through the doorway and slid along the walls to cover the prisoners completely, Nita saw the man who spoke. It was Lieutenant-governor Rixson. He stood braced in the doorway, a broad, a stubby man with a square-lined face that should have been honest, but missed somehow by the closeness of the eyes and meanness of the mouth.

"A nice bag of conspirators," he said cheerfully. "Did you think, Miss van Sloan, that you had really fooled us? Weren't you suspicious of all those patrols on the street, or hadn't it occurred to you that we could plot your movements perfectly by their reports? Yes, I think we'll wipe out the whole conspiracy tonight...."

His narrow, angry eyes swept over the men in the room. "Kirkpatrick, of course," he recognized them one by one. "Jackson, and this will be Sailor Joe... Colonel Rice." There was mockery as he called the colonel's name.

In Rice's face, Nita saw the dull, angry blood rising. The two men were strangely alike, save for that blot of dishonesty upon the face of the lieutenant-governor.

"A complete bag," Rixson said softly, "Complete except for one man, and we'll have him before the night is out if my men know anything about torture—which I fancy they do. You can save yourselves a lot of useless pain..." His face hardened and his voice snapped out, cold, incisive as a surgeon's scalpel. *Where is the Spider?*"

NITA FELT her senses reel under the impact of that question and its implication, but only for an instant. Then she laughed and her voice had the full throated gaiety of former days.

"You hear him, men?" She turned toward Kirkpatrick and the others. "You hear him? The Spider is still alive! Oh, now nothing matters! Now, we will win in spite of everything!"

Rixson took an angry stride forward, "You can't get away with any such pretense as that!" he said violently. "Wentworth has got in touch with you. We know that. All right, men, tie them up. We'll take the woman first!"

There was only a brief struggle before Kirkpatrick and the others were subdued, bound hand and foot and tossed like logs against the wall. Nita was left free, but now at Rixson's signal, two of the Black Police closed in on her. They seized her arms and, with a wrench, flung her supine upon the rough table. One of the men lighted up a cigarette.

"Now, damn you," Rixson said roughly. "You'll talk or I'll burn out those pretty eyes. *Where is the Spider?*"

Nita was afraid, but there was a warm courage in her heart that she knew nothing could touch.

"Go ahead and torture me," she said, as calmly as she could. "If I knew, I wouldn't tell you, but I swear to you that up to this minute, I, too, believed the Spider was dead!"

Rixson struck her heavily across the mouth. "Don't lie, woman," he said violently. *"Where is the Spider?"*

Nita's face went numb under the blow. Perhaps, it was the effect of that which made her think she heard laughter in the room, the flat, sinister and mocking laughter of the Spider! No, no, it was real. It had to be... No other man could make that taunting laughter; no other voice than Dick Wentworth's could speak so casually, and yet with such cold menace....

"Ask me, Rixson," said the voice. "Ask me where the Spider is… and I'll answer you with the only kind of language you can understand. A bullet through your black heart!"

And into the doorway, a sub-machine gun cradled in his steady hands, stepped… *the Spider!*

CHAPTER 4
SIX AGAINST AN ARMY

NITA KNEW a joy that was like death itself in that instant as she thrust herself up from the table and gazed once more at the man she loved—whom she now admitted to herself that she had never hoped to see again in life. The face was the sinister face of the Spider, and she saw now how thin and wasted he was with illness—but it was Wentworth. Her heart told her that… Nothing could rob him of that arrogant poise of the head, those clear eyes that were made for command.

The Black Police and Rixson must have recognized, too, that there could be no doubt of the identity of the man who challenged them. Their hands lifted like the hands of one man—all save one. A sergeant of the Black Police whipped up his revolver. Nita saw it and uttered a gasping cry. She flung herself toward him, even as she realized that she must be too late.

Something flashed past before her eyes—a glittering line of steel—and there was a thud as it struck home into the throat of the sergeant!

Nita settled back then turned her eyes away from the dying man. Of course, Ram Singh would be there in the darkness.

It was his knife that had struck home so instantly to save his master.

Nita kept her head averted while she worked carefully around the table and began to untie Kirkpatrick. There was no need for Wentworth to give the order. But she was aware of his voice, speaking rapidly, urgently, behind her, ordering the Black Police to lie flat on their faces on the floor—all save Rixson.

His voice!

"There are a few things I want to learn from you, Rixson," Wentworth was saying. "Do you think you could stand some of your own medicine? Say, a spot of torture? Your men are experts at it, and I think I could *persuade* them to invent a few new tricks to use on you. How about it, Rixson?"

Rixson answered him with an obscene curse and Wentworth took a short stride forward and struck him heavily across the mouth. "You had that coming to you, Rixson," he said. "And there'll be more. Remember, there is a lady present!"

Behind Wentworth loomed the giant figure of Ram Singh with a big automatic in his right fist, a knife balanced in his left. His teeth gleamed white behind his black beard.

"Salaam, missie sahib!" he said resonantly.

Nita shook off the daze of her surprise and moved to Wentworth's side now. The glimmering of an idea was in her brain and she rested a hand softly on his arm, stood on tip-toe to whisper in his ear. Grief stabbed her at the thinness of that arm. God, what he must have suffered!

As she whispered, Wentworth's eyes went covertly from Rixson to Rice and back again. He nodded once. Kirkpatrick, freed by Nita, had cut the ropes of the others now and they were busy securing the Black Police. Kirkpatrick came forward and held out his hand silently. There was no need for words between them. His eyes told Wentworth of his rejoicing.

"Better take Jackson and keep watch downstairs. Kirk." Wentworth said rapidly. "The city is alive with the Black Police. Rixson can't make any noise under the torture—that a gag won't muffle."

Rixson said violently, "Damn you, Wentworth! You can't get away with this! I'll see you burned alive!"

Wentworth smiled mirthlessly. "You may... if you survive. *Ram Singh!*"

Ram Singh seized Rixson by the throat and bore him back on the table, twisted his arms down so that he could not move without exquisite pain, and held him there.

"Now, Colonel Rice," Wentworth said softly, "if you would get a cigarette going...."

Colonel Rice's hands trembled as he tucked a cigarette between his square-cut lips and touched a match to it. Wentworth watched him for a long moment, then he bent over Rixson.

"I've been playing with the idea, Rixson," he said, "that you may be the Master. That was why I followed you here tonight. Whether you are or not doesn't matter now. You're in charge of the Black Police and have ordered concentration at three cities. What's the plan?"

Rixson clamped his lips shut, and Wentworth shrugged, reached for the cigarette Rice had lighted. "I've been told," he said, "that a burning cigarette in the nostril is quite painful."

Rixson's forehead was beaded with sweat. "For God's sake, Samuel!" he cried, and rolled his head toward Rice.

"For God's sake, you won't let them do this to your own brother! I saved your life!"

Wentworth straightened with a smile. "I always wondered why Rice wasn't tried with me for rebellion," he said softly, "when the Master's men arrested him in my company some while ago. So that's the answer. You're twins, aren't you Rice?"

Colonel Rice's face was totally unrelenting. "Twin brothers, yes," he said coldly. "Marvin has been a crook since we were in grammar school together. I changed my name rather than be associated with him in any way. I don't believe he's the Master, but he's capable of his crimes. And he's master of the Black Police at least." He held out the cigarette and fought hard against the trembling of his hand.

Rixson uttered a despairing cry. "All right, all right, I'll talk! We're going to loot those three cities and blame it on rebels. Listen, if you'll let me go free, I'll tell you more! The Master is going to create a diversion in Pennsylvania at the same time, to distract the federal government's attention. They've been watching us too closely!"

"A diversion?" Wentworth said softly. "A diversion of what sort?"

54

Rixson's face was dead white. He twisted his head and stared at the captive Black Police, then whispered, "There's been a lot of rain, you know. Rivers flooded. He's going to blow up the dam at the Gap."

Wentworth felt the blood drain from his own face at the revelation. In order to divert attention from his looting, the Master intended to destroy hundreds, perhaps thousands of lives. There were cities in the valley below the Gap dam. The cold-bloodedness of the thing sent a tremor through his body.

"When?" he whispered. "In God's name, when?"

Rixson was watching him, narrow-eyed now. "At midnight," he said quietly. "I don't know the method. You'll have to move fast to stop that. I could get you out of the city and give you facilities for traveling. Without me...."

Wentworth was gazing at his watch. It was ten o'clock. If he could get a plane... He smiled thinly. "Yes, Rixson, you could do all of that, if I could trust you."

"Oh, you can! I swear it!"

Wentworth shook his head, "That won't be necessary, Rixson," he said. "Colonel Rice, I think his clothes will come close to fitting you. Ram Singh will help you, if Rixson offers any objection. Nita, would you mind stepping outside...."

He closed the door of the small room on Rixson's indignant curses, and Nita was at once in his arms, "Oh, Dick!" she whispered.

WENTWORTH'S ARMS were tender about her. He held her hungrily to his heart, but there was no time even for this single stricken moment. "There was more to your idea of a rela-

tionship between Rice and Rixson, of course," he said rapidly. "I don't imagine Rice is much of an actor. He would have a hard time imitating his brother, but there's just a chance, if I had the time to coach him...."

"Then there might be a real chance of identifying the Master!" Nita whispered.

"More than that," Wentworth answered her softly. "It may

One of the bullets had touched off
a bomb in the leading ship!

enable us to take over the entire state. But that will develop later. Right now...."

"I'm not going to leave you again, Dick," Nita said firmly. "Every time we separate, something disastrous happens. I tremble to think how narrow your escape was. Your poor hands are so thin..." She drew his hand to her soft cheek, and Wentworth stooped to her lips.

"Poor child," he said gently. "You should never have met me."

Nita laughed up at him. "Oh, Grandpa, what funny ideas you have."

They stood for moments then in the half darkness of the garage, close together. For Nita, nothing now could be tragic since they were together, but she extracted the last atom of information about the days when they had been separated.

"I was hiding out the entire time in Westphalian," Wentworth told her. "The Black Police found one cellar hideout just after we'd abandoned it and that's when they faked my death. They picked up some poor devil off the street—he had a superficial resemblance to me—and murdered him!" His voice grew grim. "That's another tally against the Master to be repaid!"

"And Ram Singh nursed you back to health! He's wonderful, Dick."

"There was also a very lovely young lady named Maria Laplante," Wentworth said teasingly. "I cut her loose from a torture stake and she foolishly thought I had saved her life. She was most attentive."

"I'll scratch her eyes out!" Nita assured him savagely, and they were laughing when the sharp quick beat of feet, running through the darkness, whipped Wentworth about. He sent the light of his pocket flash reaching out, and picked up Jackson's figure.

Jackson jerked up stiffly to salute. He always used military form in addressing Wentworth, reminiscent of their years of service together.

"A company of Black Police in the street, sir!" he reported. "We're surrounded! They're not trying to get in yet…" Jackson broke off as the door of the small office opened and a man stood silhouetted against the light. Jackson's gun leaped to his hand. "Put them up, Rixson!" he snapped. "Major, the prisoner has escaped."

Wentworth laughed and the man in the doorway joined him heartily. "Good," he said, "that was all I needed to give me confidence in my imposture. What are your orders, commander?"

Jackson said, uncertainly, "What the devil…."

Wentworth studied Colonel Rice, clad now in Rixson's clothing, and nodded his head slowly. Certainly, he could pass well enough at night. By daylight, the sober honesty of Rice's face might well betray him. Make-up might help that… Hope began to lift Wentworth's heart. With Nita and these brave men at his side, what couldn't he accomplish? But there was need for haste if he was to avert the breaching of the Gap dam, and the slaughter of hundreds of innocents. Wentworth spun toward Jackson.

"You and Kirkpatrick and Ram Singh will remain within the building when we get out," he ordered. "Take all the prisoners to the hideout in Westphalian. Ram Singh knows the place and the people are friendly. Colonel Rice will join you there later. Not one of the prisoners must be allowed to escape. Rixson will be held for ransom. Get word to the state, and be careful about the method, that we demand a hundred thousand dollars ransom. Colonel Rice—" Wentworth turned toward him—"you are Lieutenant-governor Rixson for the moment. There is a company of the Black Police at the door. We'll need them for an escort… to the flying field! Once there, I'll want you to commandeer a plane for me. Let's go!"

THERE WAS a tense moment when Wentworth, his cape carefully wound about his body beneath his coat, went out through the main doors of the garage behind Colonel Rice. Nita was at his side. But the Black Police snapped to attention at sight of Rice and there was no hitch. Within moments, they were racing toward the flying field with a police escort. Wentworth began to talk in a swift undertone to Rice.

"Thanks for supporting my bluff and making your brother talk, Colonel," he said softly. "Your brother's life is, of course, entirely safe. And the ransom is a pretext. While he is held a prisoner, I want you to study his every gesture and voice inflexion. I'll be back to help you with that presently. Then when his ransom is paid, we'll release… *you!*"

Rice's heavy jaw set solidly. "You mean," he said slowly, "you want me to go to Albany and usurp my brother's position as lieutenant-governor?"

"Exactly," Wentworth told him. "And at just about that time, Governor Whiting also will disappear. You will be acting governor—in complete control of the state under the Master!"

"My God!" Rice gasped. "If I only could! We could smash this thing wide open in twenty-four hours, take back the state...."

"We could try," Wentworth said softly. "So much would depend on ferreting out the Master. If we could destroy him, the rest would be comparatively simple. It would depend on how thoroughly you can really play your brother's part."

Colonel Rice was staring straight before him, and Wentworth could see the working muscles in his jaw. The high red lights of the airport were just ahead, and the motorcycles were already shrieking out their siren warnings. Colonel Rice spoke in a voice that was strained and heavy.

"It's an enormous responsibility, commander," he said slowly. "I'll do my best!"

Wentworth said, "Good!" He clasped Rice's hand and their eyes met steadily. "I know you'll make good. I should be with you in Westphalian by morning. Good luck, Colonel."

"Good luck, commander!"

The car wheeled to a halt before the administration building of the field and one of the motorcycle police snapped open the door. Colonel Rice stepped down and, when he spoke, his voice had the harsh, arbitrary rasp of his brother.

"A fast plane, at once," he ordered. "A two-seater and see that the machine guns are fully loaded."

An officer saluted him and ran off toward the administration building and Wentworth climbed to the ground, helped Nita to alight. One plan laid, his mind was already flashing to the job ahead. Rixson had not known what method would be employed to destroy the dam and loose the flood waters on the home-crowded valley below, but the hour… Wentworth glanced at his watch. Within ninety minutes, the Master would strike. Time enough… if everything worked out precisely.

Lights sprang up in the hangar and Wentworth saw that its great open doors revealed only a few smaller ships in contrast to what he had expected. On the instant, certainty flashed into his mind that he knew the way in which the dam would be destroyed. He turned toward a near-by mechanic and waved toward the hangar.

"How long ago did the bombers take off?" he asked quietly.

"About fifteen minutes, sir," the man reported.

Wentworth swore under his breath. Moments were precious now and he dared not rush the preparations of the plane for himself lest he attract undue attention to himself and Colonel Rice. But it was quite evident that Rixson had lied about the hour set for the destruction of the dam! The bombers would quickly reach the dam and, after that, a few well-placed high explosive bombs would loose catastrophe on the valley!

Wentworth turned sharply to Nita. "We'll have to separate, dear," he said swiftly. "You'll take a second plane and carry a warning to the people. Start the telephones working—send people by auto through the valley."

Nita's eyes strained wide and dark, but she uttered no protest. Only her hand closed tightly on Wentworth's arm, while Rice ordered out a second plane. "You're going to… fight the bombers, Dick?" she whispered.

Wentworth shook his head and a grim light touched his eyes. "I'm going to destroy them!" he said quietly.

FIVE MINUTES later, his plane was taxied forward and Wentworth saluted Colonel Rice, sprang to the cockpit and whipped the ship into the air—sent it streaking wide-open into the west toward the Gap dam. Flame streaked from the exhausts and for a few moments they were plain against the night sky, like strange, fading comets. Then the blackness swallowed up Wentworth's plane.

A short while later, Nita took off in his wake. She looked back once to see Colonel Rice already turning back to his car, then her eyes focused on the black, star-speckled arch of sky before her. Somewhere out there, Dick soon would be engaging the mighty bombers of the Black Police in a battle against fearful odds. And she could not help him, could not....

Wentworth was racing desperately with time. Under wide-open throttle, the plane shivered as it sliced through the air, and ever Wentworth's eyes strained ahead for the first tracery of exhaust flame against the night that would betray the presence of the bombers. Fifteen minutes' start on a flight that you would not take more than an hour might well be fatal, for all the greater speed of the ship he flew. Wentworth strained forward, searching—searching the skies. Minutes howled past, ticked off to the roaring revolutions of his motor.

Black country and the brief, clustered lights of cities flashed past beneath him. Soaring higher, he could finally catch in the distance the row of brilliant lights across Gap dam and, behind them the glitter of their white shadows on miles of pent-up flood waters. It was no more than fifteen miles away and still no trace of the bombers! Even as the thought flashed across his mind, he saw red fire vomit up from the earth below the dam, to be instantly blotted out in roiling smoke. The first bomb!

Wentworth hammered at his throttle to gain another fraction of speed from the ship. Now, dimly, he could catch the exhaust flame of the bombers. They were at about his own altitude and were swinging in a wide circle that would bring them directly over the dam. That first bomb apparently had been misdirected and they were shifting position. So precious few seconds between safety and the death of the hundreds in the valley below! Two or three direct hits by those bombs and the entire dam would be blown out, the flood waters sent tearing over the countryside on unsuspecting people. A few seconds… if he could reach them in time!

Wentworth thumbed his gun-trips to clear them, sent a handful of bullets clawing through the night. He could see the bombers more clearly now. Three of them in a tight formation, and they had straightened out for a straight sweep above the dam. They had only to dump their loads… How many miles? Hard to estimate against the blackness. Wentworth was hurtling through space at more than four miles a minute, but it was a matter of seconds….

Once more, pointing the nose of his ship high, Wentworth thumbed home on the gun-trips and sent lead leaping ahead of him through the night. They must be out of range, but there was just a bare chance. Ah! One of the huge bombers had wheeled out of the flight and was coming back to meet him! The pilot's intention was clear—to keep Wentworth away until the bombers had finished their task.

Wentworth laughed aloud and the hammering wind gagged his mouth. There was a trembling eagerness through all his body. Enemy machine guns were spitting their venomous red fire-tongues toward him now. He eased the stick forward and plummeted beneath the attacking bomber, made no attempt to attack but raced on after the other two. They were dangerously close now to the dam.

The lights below abruptly blacked out. That was wise but tardily done. Still it might have gained him a few seconds. The two bombers released flares which plummeted down for a few hundred feet, then caught on their parachutes and, with blazing lights, drifted toward the earth. The dam was visible once more and so were the scurrying black figures that were men. Wentworth whipped up the nose of his ship to bring his guns to bear on the foremost bomber, and thumbed the gun-trips.

Even above the hammer of his engine, he could hear the staccato coughing of the guns, saw the tracers streak the air with light. His first group struck squarely on the tail structure and, deliberately, he thrust the stick forward and sent the lead searching forward through the huge fuselage of the ship. A storm of lead clawed at his own plane, beating against the wings. Wentworth held his nose steady....

Then his plane was plucked up and tossed bodily through the air. Wentworth was dimly aware of a spinning instrument board. His plane was whirling through space like a top and his senses were reeling. The night was split wide open by a white and red flame. It seemed to stand out in the blackness for seconds before it died, before the overwhelming concussion of the blast struck

Wentworth. Then even the lights were gone and he was a leaf spinning in unutterable cold space.

Through all that bewilderment and darkness, Wentworth was conscious of a small sound that was like a sob. Ultimately he realized that it was himself laughing. Numbly, his senses came back. He knew then what had happened. One of his bullets had touched off a bomb in the leading ship and both of the great planes must have been blown out of the sky.

SHAKILY, WENTWORTH fumbled with his controls, and tried to orient himself. Sky and earth wheeled about him in bewildering succession. He was tail-spinning, and the earth was dangerously close. Mechanically, still dazed by the overwhelming blast, Wentworth reversed controls. With the lumbering slowness of a truck, the ship began to answer and he swished out of the spin with the trees almost brushing his undercarriage. Zooming back toward the arch of the sky, he spotted the third bomber. Even farther from the blast than himself, the ship had gone steadily on and now, once more, it was nearing a spot from which it could dump its bombs on the dam.

Wentworth fought to get more power out of his engine, to claw his way upward to enter the battle again. He knew, even while he struggled, that he would be too late. Desperately, he pointed his guns toward the far-off ship and squeezed the trips. Nothing happened. His guns were jammed! He fought the guns while he climbed skyward and his numbed ears caught the first shattering blast of a bomb!

Wentworth groaned aloud and struggled to clear his guns. Suddenly, he saw another small plane flash across the heavens straight at the bomber. Its guns were streaking fire and the multiple armament of the bomber was answering. A second bomb made a hollow ringing concussion—then the bomber staggered! Like a wounded bird, it wheeled off to the northward above the lake and two more bombs plowed up the waters futilely. Wentworth shouted a cheer into the night. Abruptly, he cleared the jam of his own guns and they were hurling lead into the night. He was within range now and saw the second small plane swoop past the bomber with spiteful guns streaking the night with tracer fire.

Wentworth pulled up the nose of his ship and raked the belly of the bomber with lead, leveled off and wheeled upward in an Immelmann turn—whipped about and ripped lead along its back. Still the bomber staggered on. It was making a gigantic, laboring turn now, back toward the dam. Its rear guns were silent, and Wentworth climbed to dive again as the second plane whipped past to renew the attack. He caught a glimpse of an intent small face in the lights of the dash, saw an arm flung aloft in greeting to him.

"Nita!" Wentworth shouted. "Nita…" Not that she could hear him.

Once more, and a second time, Wentworth and Nita dived on the laboring bomber and, suddenly, it was no longer flying, but spinning in a flat whirl toward the waters of the lake. A blob of white flung out from a doorway in its side, but the parachute had only started to open when the man struck the water. It was only then, when the victory had been won, that Wentworth became aware that his motor was limping badly and, despite a wide-open throttle, was sagging toward the lake also!

Wentworth whipped the nose of his ship toward the shore and fought for every inch of glide he could manage. Nita's plane was hovering above him, but helpless to assist. Above the faltering of his engine, Wentworth became aware of another deeper roar. The flood waters pouring over the dam! God, had he been too late then? Had those two bombs achieved the destruction of the dam? There were streaks of white in the black water—a break in the even line of the dam's top. Wentworth groaned, set his teeth grimly as he fought the ship.

He was only a few hundred yards from shore, but there was no landing place visible. The wooded shores rose steeply. Wentworth's lips straightened into a harsh line and, deliberately, he pointed for the shallows. It meant a crash landing, but it was the best he could hope for. He began to fumble out of the parachute harness, cut the motor. Overhead, Nita's plane was very close. Her motor sounded all right. He saw a flare break from its socket under the fuselage and a moment later its brilliant light picked out the trees and the waiting waters in dazzling white and utter black. Wentworth stood, loosening the safety strap, and swung his arm in a signal to Nita.

"Go warn the people!" he shouted. "Go warn the people!"

He pointed down valley and waved her that way. There was time for no more. He swung the plane about so that it slanted to the water parallel with the shore, deliberately pulled back the stick so that it pancaked down. The impact hurtled him fifty feet through the air, but he managed to ball and hit feet first. He split the water. Its icy cold seemed to strike instantly through to his heart and in an incredibly short time his lungs were aching with the need for air. It was deep, damnably deep. He flung out his arms, stroked upward to check his descent and at long last he began to rise.

Overhead, he could make out through the water the dazzle of the floating flare—then suddenly he broke the surface. He sucked in a deep breath and struck out for the shore a short distance away. He could still hear the circling beat of Nita's engine and rolled on his back so that his white face might shine up toward her. Once more he waved his arm in a signal. The flare blacked out an instant later and then a second one illumined the surface of the lake. Afterward, the engine sound began to dwindle down the valley.

IT WAS an eternity before Wentworth could drag himself, shivering with cold, up on the stony shore of the lake. He tried to fight to his feet, but for the moment he could not manage it. He lay panting heavily, shivering with weakness. Shock and cold, on top of his enfeebled condition, had taken their toll. Only his great will still was strong. It dragged him ultimately to his feet and sent him at a shambling run toward the dam itself. It was fully a half mile away… Gradually, as he ran, Wentworth's thoroughly chilled body warmed itself. The roar of the flood waters deepened as he drew near, and fear shook him.

It was clear that the bombs had not accomplished all that had been intended, but it might be enough—more than enough! The entire structure of the dam might be weakened… Wentworth burst from the woods and ran, more steadily now, toward the powerhouse at the near end of the dam. Inside, men were working frantically by the thin light of emergency dynamos. There was a great gaping hole in the roof.

Wentworth checked at the doorway, "Did you phone a warning to the valley?" he demanded harshly.

A man with a grease-smeared face turned toward him dazedly. "Can't," he shouted. "They blew out the wires."

Wentworth groaned and walked toward them. There were only three men. The shattered bodies of others lay about.

"We're trying to get these dynamos going again," the man said dully. "If we can get the flood gates open, it may save the dam. It's… cracked."

"Aren't there any hand screws?" Wentworth demanded harshly.

The man shook his head again, "Takes two men to work one of them," he said slowly. "Only three of us. Never do it in time."

Wentworth ran to a window that showed the lower face of the dam and a shocked cry rose in his throat. One glance was enough to verify the man's words. The dam was doomed! He could see now the full damage of the bombs. The least of it was the half-moon of concrete scooped from the middle of the dam. Flood waters creamed through that break ten feet deep. It was perilous. It might close highways, but it would not doom the valley. The greater damage was below that—the crack the man had mentioned—and it was this that made the fate of the dam, of the people in the valley, so terribly sure.

That crack was already a half-foot across and, between its stone lips, a stream of water spurted straight out for fifty feet before the rising wind shattered it to spray. The pressure was tremendous. Even above the volume of the falls, he could hear the hissing of that wall of water that the lake spat out through the crack. Nothing could withstand it. Even if the flood-gates were opened at once, the dam would go, and the people below....

Wentworth wheeled from the window and broke into a run. "A car!" he ordered thickly. "Give me a car. I'll go warn the people."

The three men stared dumbly. "You're nuts," one of them said. "Absolutely nuts. You wouldn't get a mile before the dam let go."

Wentworth whipped out an automatic and wrenched the man about by his collar, drove him toward the door. "A car, damn you, or you'll go out now!" he shouted.

The man moved at a shambling run before him, fumbling for keys in his pocket. Without words, he indicated a small sedan outside the powerhouse, and Wentworth sprang to the wheel. For a numb instant, he stared at the doomed dam. As he watched, a half-ton block of concrete broke off at the lip of the crack. Like a cannon ball, the stream hurled it through space, sent it crashing among thick trees on the bank. They snapped off like clay pipe-stems.

Wentworth whipped the car in a tight turn and sent it lunging down the valley. Almost immediately, the road swooped to the water's edge. Up here, the people would be comparatively safe. A short climb would take them to high ground, but the valley spread out a few miles below and that was where the towns were situated. Thousands of people lived in them along the banks of the river, secure in the thought of the great protective dam above them—secure until the Master needed to create a "diversion!"

A furious curse sprang to Wentworth's lips. That beast must be destroyed! Too long, he had evaded justice and thousands already had died so that he might satisfy his thirst for power and gold!

Wentworth jammed the horn button with a match so that its sound rocketed continuously ahead of him through the night. He spotted a cluster of buildings about a general store, whipped out his gun and fired three shots into the air. He glimpsed a white face at a window.

"Dam's going out!" Wentworth shouted. "Dam's going out! Phone the warning ahead! Get to high ground!"

The man echoed his shout and Wentworth drove the accelerator to the floor again! The people there would be safe, but the time was so short! He could save so few lives! He was aware of the cold wind that slashed like dull knives into his pain-thinned body; of the steady rising of the ice-rimmed river that growled its increasing menace beside the road.

Ahead of him, the highway dipped still lower and flood waters were swirling across it. Grimly, Wentworth shut his lips and sent the car lunging toward the water. If it was high enough to drown out his engine, or had already carried away the road, he was finished before he had started and the thousands in the valley below were doomed! The water splashed high across the windshield. Its bitter cold touched Wentworth's body. But he had to make it. He had to....

CHAPTER 5
THE DELUGE

THE LIGHTS blacked out in Greenhaven at 11:09 p.m. On the heels of that, a low rumbling sound, that was like distant thunder, rolled down from the hills, from the direction of the dam. But it couldn't be thunder, of course. Not in the middle of winter. A few nervous people called the telephone operator for information, but no word came through from the dam. No one took serious alarm. Why should they? The dam had held in much worse floods than these—in the days before the Master.

It was curious to see the dark city, illumed only by the headlights of automobiles. The flicker of candles, lighted in the homes, was scarcely noticeable. Perhaps that was why, twenty minutes later, the plane that droned down the valley from the direction of the dam failed to spot the city and swept on past. It was about the time that its engine-beat faded out of hearing that Wentworth drove his car into the flood waters twenty miles to the north....

In the darkened Greenhaven Theater on Main Street, an audience was still waiting in darkness for the show to go on. The manager came finally to the stage and focused a flashlight on his face.

"I don't know how long we'll have to wait for the power to go on," he said uncertainly. "We can't raise the powerhouse by phone. Meantime, we'll have a little music...."

A girl came out on the stage, dipped a curtsy, went to a piano

How many hundreds had perished in the town, he dared not think.

74

and, by the light of the flash, began to hammer out a popular tune.

"All join in and sing!" the manager urged. "Come on, I'll lead you."

His voice was hoarse and tuneless and the audience laughed... and began to sing. Even if they could have heard it inside the theater, the song would have drowned out a more ominous mutter that rolled down the valley—more a disturbance of the air borne on the winter wind than an actual sound of furious waters....

"The moon was bright and yellow," sang the audience, *"When Carmen met young Manuelo...."*

But there was no moon. Dark clouds blotted it out, and an airplane was still up there somewhere, searching for a doomed town....

Twenty miles away, the fierce stream of water, jutting through that crack, tore loose another chunk of concrete. The whole dam seemed to sag a little and a little wave of water—a little wave no more than three feet high—went surging down the swollen river. Not much water, but enough to drown out a car already half submerged upon a sagging highway. It would be perhaps a half hour before that little wave reached the town of Greenhaven, but there were no lights. Perhaps, no one would notice....

The northern limits of Greenhaven were a series of small suburbs—cottage homes in the midst of friendly woods. The lights were out there, too, but in one home, the people scarcely noticed that. A fire crackled red and warm on the fireplace and a man and woman sat close together upon a davenport. In the next room, a baby fretted faintly. The woman stirred....

"That's three times now, Bob," she said. "Baby must be having a bad dream."

Bob laughed, "Silly Sally," he whispered. "Baby is too young to have bad dreams—or any kind of dreams."

Sally shook her head and pushed to her feet. "What do you know about babies?" she demanded. "People say that sometimes babies feel things that grown-ups don't. You remember, the Jacksons' baby waked them up the night their house caught fire? If it hadn't been for that...."

"Our house isn't on fire!" Bob assured her, and stretched his long legs toward the fire.

The three-foot wave of water was pushing over the riverbanks nearby, but it wouldn't reach the snug little house of Sally and Bob. It wouldn't warn them... The baby fretted again.

Sally hummed to herself as she went into the baby's room and patted its back, whispered to it one of those soft little meaningless phrases that mothers say to their infants. She was still bending over it, when the doorbell pealed. Its jangling note hammered through the still house, and kept on and on. Sally ran to the front room where Bob was on his feet. They stared at the closed door, at each other....

Bob said, "What the devil?" He strode to the door and whipped it open.

A man staggered into the hallway, a man whose green cape was black with water that dripped and dripped to the polished floor.

"Quick!" he whispered hoarsely. "Your phone! The dam is going out!"

Bob echoed his words without meaning. He peered past the man to the street and there came to his ears the distant mutter, the vibration of the air which perhaps the baby had felt. Somewhere in the distance, a dog threw a thin, wailing howl at the sky. The man in the doorway reeled, caught himself on the wall.

"The phone, you fool!" he snapped.

"In here!" Sally called. "The phone is in here. Did you say… the dam…."

"Get out of here, fast!" the man said. "The dam is going out! It may have gone already."

As he staggered forward, the cape swung out and Sally uttered a low, small cry. "The Spider!" she whispered. *"It's the Spider!"* **WENTWORTH DID** not answer her.

He was out on his feet, shuddering with cold. How long ago had his car foundered on the road? He had found a horse after that, killed it on the dash for Greenhaven. He could not feel the phone in his hand.

"Police headquarters," he said thickly. "Quickly… and tell the chief operator, the dam is going out! Spread the alarm! Blow sirens, ring bells!… Police headquarters? I just got through from the dam. It's been dynamited. It's going out. If you'll listen, you can already hear the roar of the waters. For God's sake, get the people to high ground!"

He wheeled from the phone. Sally was wrapping up the baby in a blanket. "Get to high ground," the Spider said and ran toward the door. He staggered and his shoulder caught the wall.

For an instant, he swayed there, then he bolted into the street. In the distance, a siren was beginning to wail, its note rising and falling. A church bell began a wild clangor... Wentworth began to run along the street, shouting hoarsely. He had reached the town ahead of the flood, but was there time enough?

There was a sudden, slight quaking of the ground under his feet. Even above the madness of bells and sirens, he could hear a new sullen rumble to the north. God! The dam had gone out! There could be no other reason for that sound! A motorcycle catapulted past the end of the street, siren shrill and terrible.

"The dam's going out!" the rider's hoarse voice sounded fiercely. "Get to high ground! Fast!"

A car hammered up the street, a white-faced man at the wheel. Beside him, a woman clutched a child in her arms. Wentworth saw the car stop and take on another couple at a corner, then race on. Wentworth tried to run and his feet got in their own way. He stumbled, clung to a tree, panting terribly. His eyes closed while he swayed there. His strength, drained by his long illness, had been completely used up.

Minutes dragged past while he hung on, unable to move. Children were crying somewhere near. The Spider forced open his weary eyes. A woman was running along the street, a baby in her arms. Two other children clung to the skirts of her coat. They turned in at the driveway of a house and at that moment, a car came roaring backward out of the garage. There was a man in it alone.

"Help!" the woman called to him. "For God's sake, Charlie...."

The car did not stop. It reached the street, straightened out. Wentworth fumbled an automatic from its holster, stepped into the path of the car.

"Halt!" he shouted.

He thought he shouted. His voice was no more than a whisper. The car roared toward him, unchecked. Wentworth squeezed the trigger and there was a shrill, rising scream, then the car's speed slackened. It jolted over the curb, nudged a tree and stopped.

"This way, madam!" Wentworth's voice was clearer now. "Here's a car for you!"

The woman hurried toward him with her children. "Oh," she whispered. "Oh, you… you killed him!"

"Get in the car," Wentworth said flatly.

"But I can't drive!"

Something like a groan squeezed from Wentworth's blue lips. He reeled toward the car. "Get in," he repeated.

He hauled the wounded man aside from the wheel. He was groaning, clutching a broken arm. "You murderer!" he whispered. "You murderer!"

The woman, driven by desperation, climbed into the back of the car, and Wentworth set it rolling forward along the street. Dozens of people were pouring from the houses now. Cars fled past like frightened animals before a forest fire but Wentworth stopped again and again, until the groaning auto labored and could carry no more. He found someone else who could drive, sent the car on its way. As it moved on, a woman's face showed white at the rear window for an instant and he caught the whisper of her voice.

"God bless you!" it cried. "God bless you, whoever you are!"

EVERYWHERE PEOPLE were fleeing now, but the mutter of the river was damnably close. Wentworth broke into a shambling run. He had done his utmost. He must win to high ground somehow. He must return to New York. There were three cities under threat of death tonight at the hands of the Black Police. They would be warned, but they would not know how to resist. The Master might be there. He might for once come into the open. And the Master had to die... That was the thought that kept Wentworth moving one heavy foot before the other. He staggered as he ran. He fell, and there was not strength in him to rise. He got up and went on.

A baby's wail, then a woman's voice calling to him. Wentworth heard it, but there was no response in him, only a thought. He must get clear so that the Master could be slain. Hands touched his arms and he shook them off, and suddenly a man was in front of him.

"Get into the car!" the man shouted.

Wentworth's fist knotted and somehow the words didn't make sense. He saw a fist flashed toward his jaw, felt the numbing shock of it. Only when he was falling did he realize who it was that stood before him. Somebody called Bob... He felt himself lifted and there was the hard hammer of a racing engine. People were crowded in close about him, on top of him. Wentworth tried to fight his way clear. He could get away under his own power. Some one else should have his place....

A rising scream, a scream of many voices blended together terribly, jerked him from his stupor of exhaustion. Wentworth lifted his head and found he could see out into the darkness through which they raced. He was looking at a black, high wall that was streaked with furious white. God, the flood! The wall of water from the dam! The car was laboring, was pounding under its terrific load, climbing a steep hill.

But the wall of water moved with the speed of death itself. It was reaching for them with hungry, foaming crest. It towered fifty feet high. It was upon them. It… The car seemed to leap forward. It lurched tremendously and struck, ground against a tree. Water battered against the side of the car, washed over the floor. There was a bedlam of frantic shouts, drowned out in the icy cold of the flood. Wentworth felt once more the frigid clutch of death. He fought to get his head above surface—and suddenly he was clear. He peered around, blindly.

The crest of the flood had hit and passed in an instant of mad destruction. The car vibrated against the tree where it had lodged and water still swirled above the level of the floor, but they were safe, safe… Wentworth pushed himself to his feet and climbed out. The flood sucked at him, waist-high.

"Out, you men," he ordered hoarsely. "Pass the women and children to higher ground. That tree may go."

Slowly, men answered the note of command in his voice, recognizing even in the face of death the words of a leader. They made a chain, hand-to-hand, to higher ground and along that the women pulled their way with the children. There were voices on the hill crest above them, and Wentworth's little party found its way there, toward a gleam of fire already alight. Bitterness shook Wentworth. Because he had fought his way through the black night, a few had been saved. How many hundreds had perished in the town below, he dared not think. But the Master, in spite of him, had accomplished his purpose. He had his "diversion" and back home the slaughter would go on, the slaughter and the looting....

Wentworth turned from the fire and drove his weary body on through the night. He had done what he could here—and the greater battle still lay ahead. Abruptly, he tipped back his head. A plane was droning overhead. There were fires ahead, a row of fires. As he peered upward, a landing dropped downward and burst into dazzling white light. By its illumination, he made out an open grain field ahead. He ran toward it. Nita, it might be Nita... The plane was circling lower. Before the flare blacked out, it was trundling to a halt in the field. He saw a woman's head. Thank God! Nita....

He called her name hoarsely as he ran and, moments later, Nita's arms were about him. "I warned the towns below," she said, in a dead, weary voice. "I think they got out all right. I couldn't find Greenhaven. The lights were out."

Other people were racing forward now. Wentworth heard the beat of their feet. He urged Nita toward the plane. "We've done all we can now," he said. "We'll radio a call for relief workers here, but I've got to get back to New York."

Nita let him urge her toward the plane, but she was holding back. "Must you, Dick?" she whispered. "Oh, must you? You're worn to the bone. You're wet... A flight in the plane now in this bitter cold? Surely, you can wait until tomorrow. There's so little you can do back there, one man against an entire state."

Wentworth laughed, "One man, and one woman," he said softly. "With you, Nita, I'm a dozen men in one!" He urged her to the wing of the plane. With a sigh, Nita climbed up and Wentworth sprang to the forward cockpit.

"Home, James!" he cried. "Don't worry about the wet clothes, Nita. I'll skin out of them. There's a flying coat in here and boots. Get going!" He was shuddering violently with cold. The running of people's feet was very close. "Quickly, Nita! There might be police there. After all, the Spider...."

He heard Nita's gasp, then the engine drummed out more furiously.

A TAKE-OFF in the dark was incredibly dangerous, but the trees would show blacker against the dark sky. They would have to hope that there were no boulders, no ditches in the way. The plane began to move and, instants later, Nita jacked it into the air. It lifted heavily and the black line of the trees was dangerously close before they were flying easily. But they were clear now and headed home… *Home!* Bitterness surged through Wentworth's soul. When would this grueling struggle end…?

Wentworth crouched low in the cockpit and dragged off some of his wet clothing, his soggy shoes, drew on the flying coat and boots that were stuffed into the cockpit. Slowly, his body began to warm. His eyes were burning with fatigue, but he could not afford to sleep. He must plan… His numb brain refused to work. Reluctantly, he recognized that he must rest. How many hours had it been? He slid far down into the cockpit, fastened the safety-strap and let his eyelids close. Sleep hit him like a sledgehammer....

The slowing, uneven rhythm of the motor aroused him presently and the heavy jouncing, as the plane took the earth again, brought him wide awake. He hoisted himself stiffly in the cockpit, saw the barren rim of trees about a narrow field—saw the rose-tinted edge of the sun thrusting above a blue mountain. He twisted about and looked into Nita's fatigue-shadowed eyes.

"We're about a mile from Westphalian," she said, her voice loud and uncertain because of her motor-muted eardrums.

Wentworth dragged himself out of the cockpit. The smile on his lips was gentle and vigor stirred his heart again. "I'm a brute, Nita," he said. "I should have relieved you during the night."

Nita tore off a flying helmet and shook out her chestnut curls. "You needed more rest than you got," she said. "There's a farmhouse near. We might be able to get something to eat."

Wentworth was troubled by some elusive quality in her voice, by a heaviness that refused to allow her lips to smile, but he said nothing until he had helped her to the ground and they were stumbling along on stiff legs toward the farmhouse she had spotted.

"Something has gone wrong," he said gently then. "What is it?"

Nita shook her head, "I don't know," she said. "The radio brought reports of rebellion in three cities, crushed out, and something has happened in Westphalian. I don't know what. There were four fires scattered over the town when we landed."

Wentworth accepted the news with a grim tightening of

his lips. Dashing off to save the people in the Gap valley, he had been too late to help the people in the cities the Master had selected for looting. And Westphalian... Fear touched him coldly. He had sent Rixson there a prisoner with all that remained of his gallant band. Had they walked into a trap? Unconsciously, his stride lengthened. God alone knew what new horrors the Master was perpetrating, but of this much he could be sure—that massacre of the dam had not been launched without commensurate for the Black Police.

"We've got to get back to Westphalian," Wentworth said quietly. "Rice has got to be taught how to analyze and copy Rixson's mannerisms—then I've got to go to Albany. Our plan to substitute Rice as lieutenant-governor is useless unless I can uncover the Master and destroy him."

"Yes, Dick," Nita's quiet voice was a sigh.

Wentworth glanced toward her quickly. Nita's head was bowed and her shoulders sagged with fatigue—or was it despair? He put his arm about her, tenderly.

"We'll win out, Nita," he said quietly. "We have to. Such criminals as the Master can't survive forever."

"Not forever," Nita acknowledged, "but long enough... Dick, we're in worse state than ever before. You had a small army to help you fight, now you have no more than a half dozen men. You're not even sure you have them until we learn what has happened in Westphalian.

"This plan of substituting Rice for Rixson is madness, and you know it. Suppose it did succeed for a little while? The trick would certainly be discovered within a few days, and after that, you'd be back where you started. We held New York for forty-eight hours… and the Master has it again, more tightly held than ever before. Dick, at last we've met our match. At least, we must go away until you have your strength again. Please, Dick!"

Wentworth didn't answer at once. His jaw thrust out grimly and his eyes were bleak. He realized the complete truth of what Nita said, but he would not give up. The farmhouse was before them now. A dog barked at them, backed under the porch and continued to howl his protests of their approach. A woman opened the door, brusquely ordered the dog to shut up and stood staring at them, suspiciously.

Wentworth called a greeting. "We made a forced landing in a field up on the hill," he said. "I wonder if you could give us something to eat. We'll pay you, of course."

The woman stood uncompromisingly in the doorway and continued to stare at them. "It depends," she said shortly. "People get in trouble for helping the wrong ones. Who are you?"

Wentworth laughed, "We're from Pennsylvania. There was a flood over there last night. We lost our way."

The woman stepped back and jerked her head for them to enter. "You picked a poor place to land," she said. "This is New York State."

THREE QUARTERS of an hour later, Wentworth led Nita back to the plane, and now he answered the doubts she had voiced. "All that you say is true," he said quietly, "but this is also true. I received a wound that would have killed most men—and I lived. Without reason, I abandoned a hideout—and a few hours later the Black Police raided it. More times than I can count, my life was in danger last night, but each time I survived. There is a reason for that, Nita. I am being saved for the job I've given myself—and I believe I shall succeed. Somehow, somewhere, I will find the Master—and destroy him!"

Nita refused to be encouraged, but her hand rested gently on his arm. "So long as I am with you, Dick," she said. "It doesn't matter. I'll follow you and fight with you...."

She broke off at the sound of a footstep behind them in the wood. Wentworth whirled, his hand streaking toward his gun, but it was only the farm woman. She had a dour smile on her lips.

"You didn't fool me any," she said shortly. "You're some of the rebels that are against the Black Police. Don't be afraid I'll give you away. They shot my man a month ago. But I want to warn you. There was Black Police here last night. They say there ain't a road in the state they ain't watching—nor a hiding place you people can get to. They cleaned out a rebel bunch in Westphalian last night. Seems the lieutenant-governor, that murdering Rixson was kidnapped. They got him back safe again, and bad luck to him!"

Wentworth said hoarsely, "You're sure of that?"

The woman lifted a bony shoulder. "They said so. That's all I know."

Wentworth felt the lead of despair enter his heart. Nita clung to his arm. "Oh, now there's no hope at all, Dick," she said. "We've got to escape. That's all we can do."

"Aye," said the farm woman. "That's all you can do. You better climb in that contraption and go back to Pennsylvania." She held out a packet with an abrupt movement. "Here's some lunch I fixed for you."

Nita went toward the woman impulsively, put her arms around her. "You're kind!" she cried.

Wentworth turned away heavily toward the plane. What Nita said was true. Now, there was no hope at all. Wentworth's jaw tightened, stubbornly. He would not give up the fight! His eyes fell on his hand, resting on the wing of the plane, and its gaunt boniness startled him. He touched his arms, felt their stringy weakness. In God's name, what could he do alone!

The hum of an airplane engine jerked his eyes aloft and he spotted a tight formation of fighting ships cruising high against the morning sky. Nita had thought to taxi her craft to the protection of trees before she stopped it and probably it would not be spotted. Still the planes laid emphasis on the woman's warning. All roads were closed to them—even the road to escape! With Rixson at liberty....

Wentworth swung about, "Nita, you'll have to stay here, if the lady will permit. I've got work to do."

Nita stared at him, her deep violet eyes wide. For a moment, protests hovered on her lips, but she did not utter them. Dick did what he must, and in her there could be only assent for his brave fight, however foredoomed she felt it to be.

"I'll go with you, Dick."

Wentworth shook his head. "I'm going into Westphalian. Your presence would only be an added danger."

Nita knew the reason Wentworth had given was not the true one and for a moment her jaw set in defiance. Then she softened. She must not complicate his difficulties. God knew they were strenuous enough. Presently, she watched Wentworth, in old clothing which had belonged to the farm woman's husband, drive off along the country road in a slattern car that was, literally, held together with bailing wire.

The women faced each other then; the older farm woman with her pursed lips and the scars of her years of struggle with the soil showing in her labor-bowed shoulders and her worn hands. Nita, softer, lovely in spite of fatigue and grief, but with kindness and humanity warming her face—and with her fate in her eyes. The fate of futile battles against hopeless odds, of her fruitless love for a man too chivalrous to bind her to him in marriage when disgrace and death stared him hourly in the face.

The women looked at each other and each knew the other's strength. "We'll hope it won't be a long wait," said the farm woman.

Nita smiled wistfully, "This wait, or another," she said. "What does it matter so long as he comes back at all. Oh, God help him!"

"Aye. Amen to that"

WENTWORTH BLUNDERED into the pickets of the Black Police at the very borders of Westphalian, but he had slipped into one of the disguises that never failed him—not a disguise of the face, but of the whole personality. He had become, in the interim of the drive to the town, a farmer of the rocky hills. His voice had a twang and his shoulders were stooped, his knuckles grinned.

"You going to stop us eating now?" he demanded harshly of the picket. "I just druv in to get some victuals."

The Black Police guffawed and let the old car rattle and thump its way through the streets. Lest they watch him, Wentworth actually stopped at a store and bought a supply of food stuffs. It was from a phone booth in the drugstore next door that he telephoned Maria Laplante, and, after an eternity of waiting, the black-haired girl came into the shop and made a minor purchase. She dropped a note to the floor beside Wentworth as she went out, but her eyes never touched him at all.

Wentworth stumped back to the car before he read the note and when his eyes had swept it swiftly, his face grew pale and his thin hands knotted despairingly upon the wheel.

"All your men in Concentration Camp Seven," he read. *"I'm being watched. Rixson free. Three cities sacked last night. Twenty-four men arrested Westphalian last night, taken to camp. All our leaders. Seventy-five in Albany."*

That was all, but such hell and hopelessness as those few words outlined! He was alone with a vengeance. Rice, Kirkpatrick, all of them in captivity. And the leaders… Wentworth knew well what that presaged. The Black Police were clamping the lid down all the way. Every man even suspected of subversive thoughts was being rounded up throughout the state. Twenty-four in Westphalian, seventy-five in Albany.

For a while, slumped there in the car, Wentworth fought out his bitter battle with himself. But there could be but one solution. Not resignation… but cold anger and determination to battle on until the very end!

91

How long the end could be staved off he could not know. While life was in him, he would not stop.

Wentworth kicked the old car into motion and rumbled once more through the almost deserted city streets. More plainly even than Maria Laplante's words, he read the history of the night's terror in the manner of the people. They moved along with the furtiveness of whipped dogs. A striding man in the gold-chevronned, black uniform of the Master's police walked straight down the middle of the sidewalk and, as he approached, men and women scuttled to the gutter to give him a wide berth. A child rumbled accidentally into his path and a short stick the officer carried in his hand described a vicious arc. The child screamed once, then fled in silent terror.

Wentworth was hard put to resist striking down the cowardly officer of the Black Police… yet he dared not. It would accomplish no more than petty vengeance, and it might mean the end of the Spider. And the Spider must live now. If he failed to find and destroy the Master—if he was unable to free his men from the brutal concentration camp—all was lost forever. Freedom and liberty would become terms of which the people of this state no longer knew the meaning….

Wentworth gripped the jarring wheel of the car and drove past the same pickets who had laughingly admitted him to the town… They should have stopped him, if anything could stop the Spider now. For months, Wentworth had been fighting the Master with every faculty and man at his command, but he battled cautiously for there were those he must protect. Now, even that necessity was gone.

Wentworth felt a wild recklessness in his blood and anger was cold in his brain. His mouth was a lipless gash across his hard-set face.

Tonight, he moved on Albany. Tonight, the Spider went single-handed to war against the hidden Master. He would find him. God helping, the Spider would find its prey! And then… Wentworth's head wrenched back with the force of the harsh laughter that forced its way rasping from his throat. It was flat and mocking, that laughter, strangely sinister—the laughter of the Spider whose cape cloaked the wings of Death itself!

CHAPTER 6
WHOM THE GODS DESTROY....

O N THE surface, Wentworth was calm when he returned to the farmhouse among the hills, but there was a nervous drive to his every movement that Nita recognized and which terrified her. She had seen the Spider before when cosmic anger poured its hot fire into his blood. Yet his voice was quiet enough as he told her the facts he had discovered in Westphalian.

"I want you to locate Camp Seven," he told her. "I don't know which one it is. Find out whatever you can about the locality, the time the guard changes, the number of guards and prisoners…."

"Dick!" Nita protested. "You're making excuses to protect me!"

Wentworth shook his head and his smile was almost cheerful. "Not at all. Tomorrow, or the next day at the latest, I intend to raid that camp."

"Alone?" Nita gasped.

Wentworth shrugged slightly. "Perhaps," he admitted. "There are certain preliminary steps I have to take in Albany tonight. After that, I can tell better."

Nita bowed to the mandate as everyone did when this high mood of exaltation sat upon the Spider, and he hurried off presently into the thin cold sunlight of the summer noon and sent their plane vaulting into the skies. The insignia the plane bore, stolen as it was from one of the Black Police hangars, got him past the aerial patrols, and he landed in a deserted field within a few miles of Albany. Then began the more perilous part of his trip. From here on, boldness would be his only protection. From here on, the Spider skulked no longer in back alleyways, discreetly trying to undermine the Master. Today, the Spider struck!

But first, as he had told Nita, there were certain preparations. He needed such a mirror as the Master used to transmit his commands. It was this process which had made the Master so difficult to identify. Wentworth had seized lieutenants of the Master, even the governor himself, in efforts to learn who was the Master. And all had failed because the criminal ruler of the state appeared to his underlings only as a white face in a concave mirror, speaking in a sepulchral and altered voice. Sometimes, Wentworth did not doubt, the Master himself spoke so from a mirror, but usually it was a mechanical trick of lights and phonographic attachments.

Wentworth had long ago recognized that in this device lay one of the Master's strong points—and one of his weaknesses. For others might use the same device to turn his own underlings against the Master! No doubt the Master guarded well against that weakness, but the Spider this night would break through that guard. And when he had...The Master would die! Tonight, the Spider intended to become the White Face in the Mirror and give orders in the Master's name!

Long ago, Wentworth had traced the glasses to their maker but though his men had kept ceaseless watch there, in the days when they could move freely about the state, they had never managed to ferret out the Master. Tonight, Wentworth was calling on the man, one Francis Kepler, for a different reason....

Once more, it was the toil-bowed farmer who trudged the last miles into Albany, but beneath his tattered clothes the folded cape of the Spider and the Spider's guns were concealed. He was challenged by the Black Police—and passed. It was close to the quick blue dusk of winter when he reached the remote and rather lonely section of Albany where Francis Kepler had his laboratory and dwelling. The faint warmth of the day already had faded and ice-rimmed ground was iron-hard under foot.

The farmer that was Wentworth trudged past the house and into a thicket of scrubby trees beyond. From that hideout a while later, when darkness had fallen, there emerged a quite different figure—one that moved in swift, long strides, whose glittering eyes were masked beneath the broad brim of a black hat and from whose hunched and twisted shoulders swung a long, dark cape. His body merged with the shadows of the laboratory wall near a doorway. There was brief, muted click of metal on metal and the door swung softly open.

Now....

MARVIN RIXSON

BOSS OLDHAM

FRANCIS KEPLER

Inside, there was darkness, too, save where brilliant white light shafted out beneath a door and it was here the Spider paused for a brief moment to listen. In the room, a man moved softly about to the constant tuneless whistling of a tone-deaf man. The Spider whipped out a pocket flash and shone its bright beam directly into his own eyes for a second so that the pupil became focused—then he flung open the door of the laboratory and stepped quietly inside.

"Good evening, Doctor Kepler," he said softly. "Pray don't trouble to reach for your gun. You couldn't possibly use it in time."

UNDER THE menace of Wentworth's heavy automatic, Kepler let his hands fall useless at his side. He had the keen eyes of a scientist and the tight-pressed mouth of patience. His shoulders would have been wide and husky, but long labor at his benches had stooped them. His voice came out, thin and querulous.

MARIA LAPLANTE

SENATOR McFOULARD

GOV. WHITING

"I've only got one more mirror ready," he said impatiently, "and there's no need to point that confounded gun at me."

Wentworth laughed softly, sibilantly. "One mirror will be quite enough for me, Doctor Kepler. I'll take it along." He did not put away the gun. Instead, it bore quite steadily on Kepler, as Wentworth followed him across the laboratory to a much-wrapped package against the wall.

"I'm sorry," Wentworth said then and struck Kepler lightly above the ear. The physicist pitched limply to the floor, and Wentworth stooped to bind his wrists and ankles tightly together. Afterward, he made a swift and thorough search of the laboratory in the hope of finding some clue to the Master... He failed.

Wentworth caught up the mirror and stole out into the darkness again, found Kepler's car and drove again into the concealment of the woods. There he set up the mirror and tested it, made a record for the phonographic attachment in imitation of the sepulchral voice used by the Master and then, once more, wrapped up the mirror carefully. He hid it in a thicket of shrubbery, took the record he had made and hurried across the city.

A dozen times in his swift progress, he was forced to double on his trail to avoid patrols of the Black Police and, at the delay, his anger mounted. Not exclusively because of the inconvenience to which he was put, but at thought of the terror and oppression such a patrol of the city streets indicated. Here, truly, liberty was dead! Well, it should be resurrected!

At last, Wentworth reached the house toward which he

had been making his way—the home of Lieutenant-governor Rixson!

It was a curious home for a criminal—even for a criminal who was helping to loot an entire state. Set well back from the road among thick-planted and ancient shrubs and trees, it bespoke culture and family background. Strangely, it was Rixson's own and had been in the family for years. It should have belonged to such a man as his twin brother, Colonel Rice.

Wentworth had no need to spy out his surroundings. He knew them well, and knew, too, that the house would be well guarded by the Black Police. Later in the night, he would have had no trouble entering the place in safety, but to make his way inside at this hour, not only in safety, but utterly unseen, took all of even the Spider's superlative skill.

From beneath the low boughs of a spruce tree, Wentworth spied out the location of the guards. There were two of the Black Police at the front door, two at the back, and no others. They were not too alert. Why should they be? Hadn't the last of the Spider's adherents been seized the night before and thrown into a concentration camp? What could one man do against the overwhelming force and organization of the Master? Wentworth's lips drew thin as he stole toward the glassed-in conservatory which covered one end of the house. His caped body merged with the black shadows against its wall and once more the slender lock pick of surgical steel did its work.

Moments later, he was in the humid, warm confines of the conservatory. He locked himself in, slipped toward the glass-paned door that gave on the house proper.

Through the curtained window, he made out a softly lighted library. Behind it, through a narrow arch, was Rixson's home office which was Wentworth's goal. There, he was sure, he would find the concave mirror through which the Master issued his orders—and through which the Spider would issue orders in the Master's name!

Once more a lock yielded to manipulation, and Wentworth slipped into the den. He heard a light footfall in the outer room and crouched behind a chair, gun snouting from his fist. Presently, a butler stood in the doorway. He looked about carefully, then shrugged and walked away. Probably, he had caught some half-heard sound or the scent of flower odors wafted through the temporarily opened door of the conservatory. Wentworth slowly straightened. Almost immediately, his eyes fell on the mirror he sought—set in a frame of wood built into the wall of the den itself.

WENTWORTH WASTED no time in seeking for the secret spring that might swing the mirror open. More than likely, the phonographic records the Master used were placed in the machine by some secret passageway in the walls, such as Wentworth had once discovered in the home of Governor Whiting! As coolly as if every second did *not* increase his peril a hundredfold, Wentworth set to work on the mirror. Using a small screwdriver, from a vertical pocket in a leather girdle about his waist, he rapidly loosened the frame. Now and again, he checked in his swift work to listen. He heard the measured footsteps of the butler occasionally in the hall—movements above stairs, but for long minutes he was undisturbed. Who would have suspected that the Spider labored in the very heart of the enemy forces?

Presently, the mirror panel came free in his hands, and Wentworth peered into a dark, narrow closet. Wentworth saw at once that a narrow door opened on one opposite side—either through a panel in the hallway or through some innocent-seeming closet there. Abruptly, Wentworth stiffened in alarm. Those assured and striding footsteps he heard were no butler's subdued tread! Rixson himself must be in the hallway, entering the library! With a swiftly fluid movement, Wentworth hauled himself through the mirror opening and stood in the secret closet. Dexterously, he slid the glass panel into place beneath the moldings on three sides—secured it on the fourth by thrusting a knife blade snugly home against its edge. He was not a moment too soon. A light winked on in the den, and Wentworth found himself staring directly into the face of Lieutenant-governor Rixson!

It was several seconds before Wentworth realized that while he could see Rixson, the man could not possibly see him. What he gazed through plainly was Argus glass… Rixson was smoothing his hair neatly into place. He sauntered to a chair behind his desk.

A grim smile moved Wentworth's lips. This was even better than he had dared to hope. Not only would he have ample time to plant the phonograph record he had made, but he would be able to overhear whatever was said in the den tonight. That a conference of several persons was planned, Wentworth saw at once from the arrangement of the chairs. He saw Rixson's hand go to a call button and presently a girl entered with a stenographer's notebook in her hand. Wentworth barely repressed a violent start. There could be no mistaking the girl. It was Maria Laplante, who had befriended and protected him in Westphalian! But in God's name, what could she be doing in this house as the secretary of the commander of the Black Police?

Marvin Rixson leaned toward Maria, "Have you changed your mind, Maria?" he asked softly.

Maria's eyes met his directly and there was no smile on her lips. "Have you changed yours?" she demanded.

Rixson's mouth lost its meanness when he smiled. "You're stubborn, Maria," he said, patiently. "I've got all the world in my hand, ready to lay it at your feet, and you want me to throw it away."

Maria settled herself and laid pencils in a row on the end of the desk. She frowned down at the blank pages of her notebook. "No, Marvin," she said quietly, "you're wrong. I don't care what you do with it. I'm only warning you that, sooner or later, you'll pay for your crimes...."

The butler stepped into the doorway of the den, "Governor Whiting, sir," he announced. "Mr. Daniel Oldham and Senator William MacFoulard."

Wentworth's interest quickened. He had not yet troubled to put his record upon the machine which, with a loudspeaker, was attached to the wall below the mirror. Better to hear first what the record upon it would say. Rixson obviously already knew since he had not bothered to start the mechanism... The by-play between Rixson and Maria Laplante astonished him.

Obviously, during his brief incarceration in Westphalian, Rixson had become infatuated with the brave girl who had fought beside Wentworth there. Just as obviously, Marie Laplante would have nothing to do with him—unless he quit the Master!

But her presence here belied her pretended indifference. Wentworth's lips closed grimly as he reflected that he had lost one more trusted ally. After this, he dared not trust Maria....

A slight scraping sound behind him wrenched Wentworth about in the narrow confines of the secret closet, and his hand closed warily on his gun. Was someone about to open the hidden door? Was that some one... the Master? Wentworth felt tension rip through him. He had no thought for his own danger in that confined space, only for the fact that in a moment he might be face-to-face with the author of all this tyranny. He waited tautly, but the sound was not repeated and presently Wentworth turned again to the den. But he was conscious of that door at his back. It laid a coldness along his spine like the razor-edge of an assassin's knife. God, if his presence here should be discovered, he was as helpless as a fish in a barrel. Gunshots would rip through the panels like tissue paper. There was no room to dodge, scarcely space to draw a gun....

Resolutely, Wentworth crowded the peril of his situation into the background of his mind, for all that his senses kept constant watch. He focused his attention on the den.

The men had all taken their seats, and Rixson had resigned the seat behind the desk to Governor Whiting. Wentworth knew the timorous governor thoroughly and he scarcely gave the man a glance. Senator MacFoulard he recognized at once in the white-haired pompous hypocrite near the door. He was tilted back, smoking a black cigar, frowning with narrowed eyes up at the smoke. Boss Oldham looked like a small-town undertaker, dour and long of face, with a heavy watch chain across his vest. He sat bolt upright with an air of dauntless patience, while Whiting mumbled some preliminary words.

WENTWORTH'S KEEN eyes flashed from face to face. These were the four who ruled the state and were looting it, decimating its population for their own ends. Why not, right now, blast them out of their black lives? Surely, it would cripple the Master for a while! Damn it, one of them might well be the Master himself! The man was a master at disguise as well as murder....

Wentworth found that his automatic was in his hand, the muzzle questing like a hungry hound's muzzle over the men before him. It was a struggle to force that gun back into its holster. No, he must first to be sure. These men deserved death a hundred times over, but it would be useless to remove them. He would only close the door to his one sure way of finding the Master!

Wentworth's eyes shifted beyond them to an officer of the Black Police who stood resolutely in the doorway, arms folded. There was something vaguely familiar about the man's piercing eyes. Wentworth frowned over it, then his attention was jerked violently back to Rixson. The lieutenant-governor was talking.

"The time has come for a final cleanup," he said, his pleasant orator's voice resonant. "We've got along longer than we had any right to expect, and the government can't keep its hands off much longer. We've been let alone, chiefly, because we threw up a clever smoke-screen—and because we left the big men alone. We won't any longer!"

Whiting said, worriedly, "Rixson, you're always stirring up trouble...."

"Oh, be quiet, Whiting," Rixson said shortly. "Listen..." With two long strides, he confronted the mirror behind which Wentworth stood and pitched his voice to a monotone. "White Face in the Mirror," he said, "what are your orders?"

There was a subdued clicking in the mechanism below the mirror. Lights were thrown upward and in from both sides on the concavity of the mirror and Wentworth knew that they were forming a shadow face there. From the loudspeaker, sepulchral and unearthly, came the voice of the Master!

"Clean out every man even suspected of having the brains to cause trouble," the Master ordered harshly. "Send them to concentration camps and kill them with the plague. Organize your forces and, in twenty-four hours, loot every bank and wealthy man in the state. The time has come for a final clean-up. Prepare your plans. I will name the hour within two days!"

Wentworth choked down the harsh oath that leaped to his lips as the voice ceased. The sheer enormity of the calm proposal for massacre was a profound shock even after these months of dealing with the merciless Master. Wentworth's fists knotted furiously at his side. By the heavens, these men should die now! No, no. Not yet. Not until he had set his own plans into operation.

Shuddering with the effort at control, Wentworth silently

removed the played-out record from the machine and substituted his own. Immediately, he knew that he had done something wrong. Scarcely had he slid the cylinder home when the lights blinked on again. The men in the room whirled tautly toward the mirror and Wentworth heard his own voice, in tones that matched those of the Master, issue new orders....

"I have received information," it said, "that a rebellion is planned here in Albany. Summon all Black Police here to the city at once at top speed. It is our only chance!"

For a moment, the men in the room stood in shocked tableau, then at the door, Wentworth caught a flash of movement. He saw the Black Police officer whip out his revolver and, even as Wentworth stared at him, the man drew a deliberate bead on the Spider! It was exactly as if, for him, the Argus glass offered no block to vision. His muzzle held unwaveringly on Wentworth's heart. The trigger finger was whitening with pressure....

Wentworth twisted frantically in the narrow closet and wedged himself toward the floor. He was not an instant too soon. The crash of the gun was an echo for the falling clatter of the bullet-smashed mirror. Wentworth had his gun in hand while he groped behind him for the fastening of the secret door. He must be swift. Within moments, the bullets would comb every inch of his narrow prison, and....

A jagged oath tore at Wentworth's throat! He was a fool! But it might not be too late! Wentworth held a gun in each hand, and he had not fired. He had seen the Black Police officer and felt his familiarity, and he had not killed him.

It was only now he realized that… the Black Police officer was the Master himself!

CHAPTER 7
TO THE DEATH!

WENTWORTH STARTED to straighten to the attack and, near his face, a heavy bullet punched through the wooden panel, gouged splinters into his cheek. Another plucked through his hat. Wentworth's face set in grim justice's mold, did not change. He should have recognized at once the meaning of the attack by the Black Police officer. Any one of the men in the room might have known that the closet was there, but only the Master would know that he had never dictated words uttered by one White Face in the Mirror. Or he must have figured that the Spider must be within the closet to change the records at that precise moment. Yes, it was typical of the Master's swift mental processes to figure matters out in such split-second style and to open fire at once!

Even as these thoughts went flashingly through his brain, Wentworth knew that he could stand no chance of shooting it out successfully with the Master unless he escaped from this closet that well might become his coffin. Only instants of time had elapsed since that first shot—only time enough to fire two more. And each of those had narrowly missed killing the Spider.

With the thought, Wentworth braced his shoulders against the small secret door, thrust violently with his powerful leg muscles—and crashed supine into the hall! He had a glimpse of a white-faced butler, rigid against the stair; saw plaster dust fly as bullets ranged through the closet and buried themselves in the wall. Then Wentworth was up and darting for the hallway's arch to the library and the den. It was one man against five, but one of the enemy was the Master! To reach him, Wentworth would gladly battle his way through an army!

There was a great bounding joy in Wentworth's heart. Nothing mattered save that, at last, he was to meet the Master face to face. He bounded into the library and gunshots streaked at him from the darkness of the den. He laid his bullets along those lances of flame and a man cursed in a thin, broken voice and afterward the fall of his body jarred the floor. Governor Whiting was pleading for protection. His whining was the only sound through a long dark moment while Wentworth crouched with his restless guns questing about him. He could plainly see the lighter squares of window doors. If anything moved against them....

A whistle skirled an alarm, or a command, and the building filled suddenly with the tramp of many running feet. The Black Police guards had been called in to exterminate him. Wentworth laughed silently. Before they could strike, his work would be finished. He straightened and went on soft, long-striding feet to the entrance of the den. His hand found the light switch! With one movement, he flicked it on and hurled himself aside, ready to shoot.

One man lay prone on the floor, a gun beside his hand. It was Senator MacFoulard. Governor Whiting was crouched behind desk and chair, still pleading for succor. There was no one else at all in the room! Anger shook Wentworth. He smacked out the light as bullets threshed across the den.

Whiting's pleading became screams but Wentworth was diving toward the mirror's opening and the closet. That way the Master, Rixson and Oldham must have fled. The feet of the charging Black Police were tramping across the library. Their flashlights slashed the gloom… but the Spider was swift and silent. An instant before they entered the den, he was stepping quietly into the hallway. He closed the narrow secret door behind him, strode toward the butler.

"Where did they go?" he demanded harshly.

It was only then that he saw the man's arms doubled across his stomach. As Wentworth spoke, the man's eyes rolled up, his knees gave and he slid, twisting, to the floor! His arms fell aside and there were gaping red holes in the white vest. The curses of the Black Police, their running feet, were moving back toward the hallway now. Wentworth had a space of seconds to make his decision, but he reasoned coldly.

The Master and his allies had had no chance to get past him in the front hall. They could have only fled rearward. If they had left the house, they were beyond pursuit, but there was a cellar… Wentworth's lips moved in a hard smile. Even in their fear of the Spider, he doubted they would have fled from the house. They would be too anxious to make sure that their last potent enemy was slain! Surely, then, they were hiding in that basement!

Wentworth reached the doorway in two long bounds and whipped the door open… but did not stand in the opening. Silence and blackness below—no more. Wentworth lay prone on his stomach and made two, then three steps creak with the pressure of his hands as if a man crept down them, and still there was no response from the basement. Wentworth frowned, but did not doubt his reasoning.

He eased onto the steps, drew the door shut and, head-first, crawled down the stairway until cold concrete touched his palm. Wentworth was smiling now. The enemy were here. He could feel their presence, could almost hear their close, fast breathing. Softly, he moved around until he crouched behind the steps, his guns in hand. Then he settled himself to wait… to wait while overhead the wild search of the Black Police made the house shake, while their blood-thirsty shouts echoed about him. Let him find and slay the Master and he would take his chances with them!

ABRUPTLY, WENTWORTH caught his breath. He had heard a soft, metallic click that might be the cocking of a gun—or might be the closing of a door! He whipped out his flashlight, held it at arm's length above his lowered head and squeezed out a brilliant shaft of light.

In one swift sweep, it circled the basement—and found nothing! Yet they had been here. Wentworth knew it. Some secret

NITA VAN SLOAN

door… Instantly, Wentworth was on his feet, questing over the cellar. There was not an opening of any kind that he could detect, not even a window. The walls were thick stone and gave back steadily the sound of solid masonry….

The voice that spoke to him was quiet, mocking. Wentworth whirled, his light questing, but found only a small loudspeaker placed high against the rafters.

"Congratulations, Spider," came the mocking voice of the Master. "You did well to escape the closet. Fortunately, the walls here are a bit more solid. But I won't risk my men to remove you. It isn't necessary in the least. If you'll listen carefully, you'll hear the hiss of gas. Phosgene, Spider. If you survive for five minutes, you will greatly surprise me. Still, you are intelligent. I conceded that. Say, five minutes... I shall miss you, Spider. You have made things... interesting. But I shall soon be through here. Good-by!"

Wentworth did not move until he heard the click which meant the microphone was dead. He flung a single swift glance up the stairs. There would be Black Police up there, but not the Master. He had spoken from whatever secret passage led out of the basement, and that was the way the Spider would flee! There was actually a smile on the Spider's lips as he set swiftly to work.

He poured the contents of a tiny vial of fluid, drawn from a pocket of the girdle, upon a handkerchief and bound it tightly over nose and mouth. It was a gas neutralizer, designed chiefly for use against tear-gas but effective against others to some extent. Against phosgene... Wentworth's eyes were narrow and hard. He did not know what it would accomplish against phosgene, one of the most deadly gases contrived by man. Seconds were precious....

Wentworth closed his eyes and, in imagination, brought back that faint click he had heard in the darkness. He held his gun in his hand, for he knew that his instinctive pointing of the weapon, trained through long years of life-and-death struggle, would be more accurate than any logical placing of the sound by mental processes. He opened his eyes then and found the gun centered on the remote corner of the room. Wentworth swore under his breath—for it was from that corner, too, came the hiss of escaping gas! He was right, but any attempt to reach the wall might well prove fatal!

Wentworth's lips closed thinly. To hell with that! He was going through… Swiftly, he surveyed the wall. He tapped there with the gun butt and found it solid. Any opening of the wall then would be by means of counterbalance which meant, undoubtedly, that the section of wall which constituted the door would sink through the floor. He had to look then for a catch which would be released near the ceiling. Possibly the weight of his body, pressing down, would be sufficient to thrust the section of wall down….

With the thought, Wentworth sprang into action. There were water pipes overhead—cross-braces between the rafters—and phosgene was heavier than air though it took a very small admixture of the gas with air to make it lethal. The fact that the air of the basement was dead and would not circulate helped him some. If he were swift… With a lithe leap, Wentworth reached a water pipe and swung, hand over hand, along it, directly toward the corner where the gas escaped!

When he reached the corner, he swung up his knees and dangling by one hand only, flashed on his light. It swept minutely the juncture of floor and wall, and he smiled thinly. Figured logically, it was easy enough to locate the space where the door opened. The gas was escaping from the narrow crack beneath it. Wentworth turned his attention to the top of the wall to find the catch that would hold it in place against the counterbalance. With his screwdriver, he prodded into the cracks….

WENTWORTH'S EYES were burning and he was dizzy from the suppression of breath. He dared breathe only when he absolutely must, and then lightly. For long, dragging seconds, he forced himself to take in no air at all. The screwdriver grated on rock, slid from crack to crack, but nothing happened. No obstacle appeared that might be the catch. Wentworth found his movements becoming frenzied and deliberately stopped all action for a count of ten.

He peered at the wall then, thinking… thinking. He could not accidentally hope to find the catch. It must be done by reason… Abruptly, he reached out to the wall and threw his pressure upon a single rock. It did not yield. With the close white beam of his light, Wentworth studied the mortar between the rocks. His brain was reeling now from suffocation, his eyes starting from his head. And the gas… How long had the Master said. Five minutes? But probably, he had deliberately set the period long to lull the Spider into inactivity until too late.

Wentworth shook his head, stuck doggedly to his task. Finally, his searching eyes found what he wanted—not in the door itself, but in the wall beside it. A few flecks of mortar clinging to the rock-face, a slightly crumbled crack….

His fingers and knees were slipping from their grip on the pipes. He could scarcely see for the black pounding of suffocated blood behind his eyes. The hand he reached out to the rock trembled, but, by a supreme effort, he threw all his weight behind the thrust He felt the rock yield fractionally, then it moved inward a half inch and he heard once more the faint click that had come to him through the darkness. Instantly, a section of the stone wall slid downward on smoothly oiled counterbalance and the next instant, Wentworth had hurled himself into the black passageway that was revealed!

A cool draft blew against Wentworth's face as he ran and there was a prayer of thanksgiving in his heart. That draft would hold back the awful gas that was filling the basement behind. The stone door already had slid back into place… Wentworth checked himself, listening intently. No sound reached him here—nothing at all stirred save the draft, cold against his face. He crept on more cautiously and now the gun was ready in his fist. Now and again, he sent the beam of his flashlight questing ahead. Only the narrow, dark walls of the tunnel showed, stretching ahead. He found the tank from which the gas issued and a microphone beside it. A dozen yards beyond, rough wooden steps led upward. A trap door was half-open.

For an instant longer, Wentworth crouched on the steps, listening. There was a mad urge in him to fling himself out into the open, to risk whatever bullets might fly in the mad hope of catching the Master. Reason dictated that the Master had long since fled the place. He was no more accustomed to revealing himself, in person, to his allies than to his enemies… Cautiously, Wentworth lifted the trap-door and found himself in an empty garage. A bitter curse fell from his lips, but only one. He had failed!

He had been face-to-face with the Master and had failed! His plan, too, to concentrate the Black Police, and hence weaken the guards of the prison camps, had gone awry. He could not delay for that reason. He must forge ahead more strongly than ever before. Within two days, the Master had said, he would order the wholesale massacre and looting of the state. Now that he knew his plans had been overheard, he would make every effort to speed the blow. And the Spider was alone, one man against an army.

It was time indeed for desperate measures! Wentworth drew in a deep, slow breath. Perhaps, desperation might win where long and faithful effort had failed. Perhaps… but Wentworth had only the hope that comes to men when death is near, the last frantic clutching at straws. Not that he would fight less hard because he realized how faint was his chance of success! That was not the way of the Spider!

Two paths only were open to him. He could remain in Albany and institute a Spider's reign of terror—strike down the leaders of the criminals—or he could free his men from the concentration camp to which he had sent Nita as a spy, and put Rice in as the double of the lieutenant-governor. No man realized better than Wentworth the obstacles to both plans. His reign of terror could no more than begin before the massacre was launched. On the other hand, Rice could not hope to escape detection for long, even supposing Wentworth was fortunate enough to free him from the camp and to put him in Rixson's place without arousing suspicion….

Something very like a groan forced its way out between Wentworth's set teeth. Despite the difficulties, the plan that involved Rice was better. It alone offered any hope of permanent relief from the Master and his hordes. If they could hold control of the state for a few hours and issue orders which would command the prompt obedience which the Master obtained through fear!

Slowly, Wentworth nodded. That was what he must do, and the first step was... to deliver Rice from a concentration camp. A small smile played around Wentworth's lips. Even with a body of armed men, that would be almost impossible now since Wentworth's previous raids had caused increased strength of fortifications and guards. Single-handed... The smile stiffened into a grimace of determination. They could not stop him now! They could not....

SWIFTLY, BEFORE the Master and his allies should discover the escape from the basement, Wentworth fled the neighborhood of Rixson's home. He went back to Dr. Kepler's stolen car and, at various filling-stations, bought gallons of gasoline in cans to refuel the plane. He still had need of that. Wentworth's mind was working at top speed now. Already, he had a glimmering of an idea for forcing the camp, and he would need the plane for Rice's escape to Albany! So, two hours after his escape from the basement, Wentworth was winging his way back toward Westphalian again. A quick landing there and once more he was entering the beleaguered town. There were certain preparations to be made before he could raid the camp!

On a dark side-street, he waylaid one of the Black Police and swiftly donned his uniform. Then, carrying an order he had forged, he went to the central armory of Westphalian. Within another hour, he was driving from the city a huge truck loaded with mining supplies, among which were three boxes of dynamite! Back at the farmhouse in the hills, he found Nita just returning wearily from her survey of the camp. She flung herself into Wentworth's arms.

"Oh, Dick!" she cried. "I was sure you had met trouble in Albany!"

Wentworth laughed gently. "I met trouble... but it got away from me. The camp, Nita?"

"Impregnable," she said wearily. "There are easily two hundred Black Police on guard with perhaps a thousand prisoners. There are five concentric fences around the camp, two of wood, three of barbed wire. The middlemost one is charged with electricity, a killing voltage."

Wentworth nodded, his eyes intent and eager. "When do they change guard, Nita?" he asked. "Say, at dinner hour at night and in the morning, are all the Black Police assembled?"

Nita nodded. "They certainly are at night. All the prisoners are lined up against one side of the camp. The guard changes on the opposite side, near the gates. They make the prisoners stand at salute almost an hour while some are disciplined. I... I heard a man flogged to death!"

"Sleep now, dearest," Wentworth admonished Nita. "At dawn, take the plane—it's been refueled—and fly to the most convenient hidden field near the camp. When you hear shooting, send up a rocket—I have some in the truck—so that I'll know where you are. I'll do the rest!"

Nita's tired face became more drawn, "You're going to try to deliver those prisoners," she said woodenly.

Wentworth bent to her lips, tenderly. "No, darling, I'm going to deliver those prisoners. I must, or…" He let the sentence trail off. "Sleep until dawn, dearest."

"But you, Dick!"

Wentworth shook his head. "I have some supplies to deliver to Concentration Camp Seven. It's a longish drive!"

He gave Nita the supplies she needed, loaded down the farm woman with foodstuffs and, fifteen minutes later, was rolling off through the hills, still clad in the uniform of the Black Police. At dawn he stopped on the crest of a ridge and peered down into the wide, flat valley beyond. The concentration camp sprawled in its midst, without a tree, with only the rude hovels the prisoners had built themselves for protection against the bitter cold.

Wentworth himself was muffled in a heavy overcoat with thick gloves on his hands. In the frigid dawn, his breath made a white cloud like steam, as he labored over the boxes of dynamite and lengths of fuse and wire. When, presently, he heard the thin strains of a bugle in the camp, he climbed back to the driver's seat and started the truck lumbering downgrade. Its speed mounted steadily.…

IN THE concentration camp, prisoners were being routed from their meager beds into the deathly cold. There were some, as every morning, who did not rise—who were beyond the cruelties of the Black guard, but the others rose, shivering, to stand in ragged lines at salute while the guard changed.

The Black Police were muffled to the ears in impressive uniform overcoats and even so there were men among them who grumbled as they took their places in line. The entire company was formed up save for those who kept watch from the machine-gun towers about the camp. One of these men caught up a phone that communicated with the gate.

"Supply truck coming," he said lazily, "and tell the cook to damn well hurry my breakfast up here. I'm hungry!"

The gate guard snarled back at him. "Starve, damn you! That watch tower is heated. I got to stand out in the cold."

The rumble of the truck was loud. Plainly, the driver was in a hurry to reach shelter, too. He was driving with a wide-open throttle, and the heavy truck swayed as it hammered along the straightaway that ran directly to the gates through the multiple fences. Just inside the gates, the companies of the Black Police were formed up while the commander read out the orders for the day—and the punishment. One man was to be flogged before breakfast.

"God almighty," groaned one of the gate guards. "Now we got to wait until that damned punk dies. I hope he dies quick!"

The prisoner was marched out from solitary confinement in the cellar below the comfortable quarters of the troops. He was naked to the waist and shuddering with the cold. There was a bloody tear on his left bicep, an old wound, but his shoulders were well back and his soldier's head was carried erectly.

"Nuts," said the guard, "that one will be slow dying. It's that rebel, Kirkpatrick."

He was trussed up to a cruciform post, arms strained high, and the torturer stepped forward with his heavy whip. The roar of the truck was very close now. The gate guard turned that way sullenly, looking back over his shoulder as the whip swung through the air for the first slashing blow.

The guard touched his lips with his tongue, as the gashes cut by the thongs showed red against the white flesh. Then he looked toward the truck... His eyes stared abruptly wide.

He couldn't see anybody at the wheel and the truck was racing with tremendous speed straight for the gates, and less than a hundred feet away. The guard let out a strangled cry of amazement—and in the interim the truck covered the last hundred feet.

The steel gratings of the outer gate burst open with a report like a gunshot and were ripped bodily from their hinges. One of them caught a guard and tossed him, a broken thing, onto the barbed wire of the second barrier. The truck, with the huge momentum of its speed, the tons of weight of its body and load behind it, did not even hesitate.

It rammed through the second gate, the third, then whanged against the innermost barrier. This was a gate of steel, also, heavier than the outer portal, and strongly braced. Against it the truck lunged with an almost living fury. One of the gates ripped loose from its upper hinge and slammed flat down on the ground. A squad of men was caught beneath it. They did not have time even to scream before they were ground to pulp beneath it. The truck jounced up on the steel ramp the gate formed, trundled more slowly forward and rasped to a halt against the solid brick masonry of the gate post.

Inside the concentration camp, bedlam had broken loose. At the guard's first shout, the officers had stared toward him. Before they could even shout an order, the inner gate had fallen upon the close-pressed ranks of the guard and killed a dozen. Men began to scatter, but the stern orders of the officers, the crack of a revolver that blew down a fugitive, whipped them back into line.

"Close the gates!" rang out the order of the commander. "Haul that truck inside!"

In response to his shouts, the Black guard converged on the truck while the prisoners still stood in ragged, shivering files. One of the Black Police reached the running-board and clambered on it. Other men swarmed up behind him. It was precisely sixty seconds since the truck, with a peculiar, wired contrivance on its bumper, had struck the first gate. Wentworth had done his timing well and he had calculated properly. As the last of sixty seconds dribbled past, the dynamite let go. It caught the Black Police at the time of maximum concentration about the truck....

FROM THE ditch outside the camp into which he had thrown himself, Wentworth saw the up-thrust spires of scarlet and livid flame, saw the black whirling fragments of men tossed high against the sky. What remained of the gates and the posts beside them was blown outward, and Wentworth knew that the front end of the truck had exploded like a huge grenade, hurling jagged fragments among the close-packed police. Wentworth saw one wheel soar like a well thrown discus through the air and sail out beyond the confines of the camp. It bounced a full fifty feet into the air before it fell again and quivered to a halt like a spun coin.

The instant the concussion of the blast had swept past him. Wentworth was on his feet and running toward those shattered gates. An automatic was in each fist and his eyes swept the machine-gun towers. One of them had been shattered by a high-flung fragment of the truck... but there were three others. As soon as the men got over the stunning force of that explosion... *Ah!* Wentworth spotted movement inside the nearest tower and his guns blasted in unison. His deafened ears barely heard the shots, but he saw that the white face he had glimpsed, a moment since, was hammered out of sight.

Wentworth scrambled across the huge crater where the truck had stood and ripped off the overcoat and uniform cap. From his shoulders fluttered the green cape of the Spider.

"Citizens, arise!" he shouted clearly. "Overthrow the tyrants! The Spider has come to save you!"

For an instant, those shivering ranks of men stared at him, motionless, as they had stood through even the terror of the blast. They had felt the iron hand of discipline so long! But at sight of Wentworth, a mutter stirred through them. Then, as a wave breaks on the rocks, those lines shattered and the men charged forward. Some of the Black Police were still on their feet, though dazed by the enormity of the disaster that had struck them. They did not survive the charge. One of the machine guns stammered from a watch tower and cut a bloody swathe among the prisoners. Instantly, a dozen men were swarming up into the tower and soon the gun was still.

Wentworth spotted the tortured Kirkpatrick at once and ran to him with the overcoat he had discarded, laid it tenderly about the lacerated shoulders before he slashed loose the bonds. There was a thin, bitter smile on Kirkpatrick's lips.

"You didn't come too soon, Dick," he said crisply. "They were going to flog me to death before breakfast."

Wentworth cursed harshly. "Rice is still alive?" He scarcely dared voice the question.

"Alive, yes," Kirkpatrick said slowly. He winced as he put arms into the coat-sleeves. "He got a bullet through the side when we were captured. I haven't seen him since. What now, Dick... Another march on New York?"

Kirkpatrick's voice sounded hopeless. God, if these camps could break the spirit of such men as Kirkpatrick! Wentworth peered at him, but did not voice his thought. And yet, he could not blame Kirkpatrick. He had been so hopeful when he had been restored to power in New York City as police commissioner, and nothing had come of it—nothing save flight and disaster.

"No march, no," Wentworth said shortly. "Take me to Rice and the others!"

The worshiping eyes of freed men followed Wentworth, as he strode toward the barracks building with Kirkpatrick. One man, thickly bearded, clad in rags, sprang into Wentworth's path. "I was your man, commander," he said hoarsely, "until the battle in Westphalian. They caught me after that, and by God they've made me suffer. With you to lead us...?"

Wentworth recognized the man with difficulty through the lines that suffering had gouged into his face. "You shall lead them Stevens," he said quietly. "You've seen how I smashed open this camp. There will be dynamite here. Steal trucks and attack the other camps, if the men will follow you—and I think they will. I have a job to do. If it succeeds...."

Stevens laughed hoarsely, "It will succeed, commander!" he cried. "You can't fail!"

Wentworth clasped the man's shoulder and strode on. He couldn't speak for the thickness that closed his throat. If only their faith in him was justified. "I can't fail," he muttered to Kirkpatrick.

Kirkpatrick looked at him curiously, "I don't believe you can, Dick," he said quietly. "Not in the end."

Wentworth laughed harshly and made no answer. Hadn't he had the Master under his gunpoint and let the man escape him? Never would he find the Master again in the identity he had assumed last night. No, it was all to do over again. If only Rice was strong enough... Cell doors clanged open under Wentworth's hand and he strode down the line of dark dungeons with their solid doors, throwing them wide open to free the wretches within. He found Jackson, Ram Singh, their faces haggard with starvation. Sailor Joe had almost lost his smile and Rice....

Wentworth stared down at the wreck of a man on a cot and saw the collapse of his plans. Rice managed a smile. "It's not as bad as it looks, commander," he said, "but the devils wouldn't patch up the wound—and they haven't fed me."

WENTWORTH PERMITTED a single jagged oath to escape his lips. Rice's indomitable courage would undoubtedly pull him through, but there was no time to doctor up his strength. Already twelve of the maximum of forty-eight hours the Master had allowed were elapsed, and he had reason to know that the Master would rush his plans now. At most, twelve more hours remained to him. Wentworth swung from the cot.

"Ram Singh, cleanse and bandage the wound," he ordered. "Jackson, rustle food. Sailor Joe, Miss van Sloan has an airplane in the field a mile up the road and perhaps three hundred yards to the right. Take a car. Ask her to land as close to the fences as possible. We'll take off in about an hour. Now, Colonel Rice...."

"Dick," Kirkpatrick interrupted. "If you don't need me, I'll get these poor devils upstairs organized and under way. They'll be slaughtered if they're caught here."

Wentworth nodded, his eyes never leaving those of Rice. Swiftly, he outlined to the prostrate soldier the details of the Master's plans. "Only one thing can stop them; only one man," Wentworth told him with slow emphasis. "If you can take Rixson's place and hold it for a few hours, we can disrupt their organization—perhaps disband the Black Police. If then, we could eliminate the Master, you might continue the masquerade until the entire state was on its feet again. I can't overemphasize the risk, but it's the only way open to us now."

Colonel Rice's gaunt face twitched at Ram Singh's ministrations to his wound, but he nodded. "You know, Wentworth, that anything I can do, I will. If you could stick with me and instruct me as we go along, I think perhaps we can do it. But how will you install me in Rixson's place?"

Wentworth said, "I have a plan!"

An hour later, the camp was cleared of men and with the pale, but strengthened Colonel Rice, Wentworth hurried to the two-seater plane which Nita had brought close against the fence.

Nita's face was white, her eyes large and dark—"You let the prisoners go," she said. "I thought you'd use them as an army…."

Wentworth shook his head curtly. "We tried that once before—and the federal government chased us out. We're going to try what's known, in the banana republics, as a 'palace revolution.'"

"And my job?" Nita asked quietly.

Wentworth smiled at her, "Your job will be even more dangerous than mine, dear," he said softly. He turned to Kirkpatrick and threw his Spider cape about his friend's high shoulders. "You two must distract the attention of the Master, of the Black Police, and make them believe that the Spider freed his men only to harry them. Fight the Black Police at every turn, try to prevent them from taking prisoners, free chain-gangs and stop lootings. Go everywhere and sprinkle Spider seals over the face of the map,"

"But you, Dick!" Kirkpatrick and Nita spoke together.

Wentworth still smiled. "Colonel Rice and I are flying to Albany… to stage our palace revolution!"

Moments later, Wentworth whipped the plane from the earth and sent it roaring toward Albany, and his eyes were bleak.

Those others, his friends and allies, were encouraged because of his feat at the camp, but Wentworth knew that this was nothing compared to the problem that lay ahead!

CHAPTER 8
RED CHALLENGE

I N AN hour, Wentworth set the plane down on the official Black Police airfield at Albany. He was once more in the uniform of an officer, of which there had been many at the concentration camp. Colonel Rice, unshaven, but otherwise well enough dressed, had his hands handcuffed before him and Wentworth kept a drawn gun in his hand.

"Special prisoner for the commander," he told men at the airport curtly. "Orders to take him directly to the commander's home."

He showed a written order which he had prepared and, within minutes, was roaring off to Rixson's home with a full police escort. He managed to get rid of them at the entrance of the grounds and then hurried, on foot, directly to the house itself. Colonel Rice kept his head bowed, his shoulders sagging with weakness as Wentworth directed. It was no part of his plan that the resemblance between Rice and Rixson should be detected, and he was gambling that Rixson would not be at home....

The butler opened the door to his peremptory ring, and Wentworth's eyes shot beyond him to the library and the den. They were empty, so far as he could see, and Wentworth checked a breath of relief.

"Prisoner for Commander Rixson," he snapped at the butler.

The man shook his head, "The lieutenant-governor isn't home," he said, "and...."

Wentworth thrust Colonel Rice forward into the hall. "Then we'll wait," he said shortly. "Give me a room for the prisoner and notify the commander. Important prisoner from New York City, by special order!"

Wentworth's heart was bounding with hope. He had calculated correctly so far. If Rixson was unsuspicious and came home at once, without too many men... The butler bowed before his commanding manner and gestured him up the stairs. Wentworth thrust Rice that way with his ready gun, started up after him—and heard light quick footfalls in the hallway above. Wentworth's eyes jerked that way, and tautness raced over his body. Peering down at him was Maria Laplante!

Wentworth paid no attention to her, apparently, but he hurried Rice in his climb of the stairs and he made his own carriage a feigned swagger. There was a strong possibility that she would identify him, and there was no way of telling what her reaction would be. Though she had never betrayed the Spider, it was plain that she was very fond of Rixson and that fact made her damnably dangerous at this moment. One word of alarm from her now... The butler was calling up the information that Wentworth had given in answer to Maria Laplante's quick challenge.

"Stumble and fall!" Wentworth whispered to Rice.

Immediately, Colonel Rice tripped and pitched prone on the steps. Wentworth ripped out an oath and, apparently, drove his toe hard into the fallen man's side.

"No tricks!" he snapped. "One more like that, and I'll blow your spine in half!"

Maria Laplante came rapidly down the steps toward him and bent over the fallen man and, in that instant, Wentworth leaned close and jabbed the gun muzzle into her side.

"Not a sound, Maria," he whispered. "The Spider speaks!"

He felt Maria Laplante stiffen under the prod of the gun muzzle, but she was obedient. She helped Rice to his feet, "Oh, you poor man!" she said gently. "Are you hurt?"

Wentworth moved warily close to her as they climbed the steps and turned finally into a corner room. Wentworth whipped the door shut then, and Maria Laplante whirled toward him, her dark eyes angry and hurt.

"Do you have to hold a gun on me?" she demanded sharply. "Are you forgetting that I once saved your life at the risk of my own?"

Wentworth smiled at her, his eyes keen and searching. "No, Maria," he said gently, "but I'm not forgetting either that all this was before you met Marvin Rixson. It is a little... strange to find you here."

"Your cause was lost," the girl said with a toss of her thick black hair. "I tried to win by my own methods, to persuade Marvin Rixson to—" she glanced nervously about, changed to a whisper—"turn on the Master! Why are you here? I'll help you do anything, anything at all, except...."

"Except harm Marvin Rixson," Wentworth finished quietly. "Yes, I know. He won't be harmed, but I intend to hold him a prisoner in this room for a few days. After that—" he shrugged. "—we may all be dead."

Colonel Rice was watching the two of them keenly, "Your

best guarantee that Marvin won't be harmed is this," he said to Maria. "Marvin is my brother."

Maria Laplante's eyes swung to him, probed keenly into his face. Abruptly, she sucked in her breath. "Oh, I understand now. I see the resemblance. You… you are going to be the lieutenant-governor!" Neither man answered, watching the girl closely. Maria began to smile, then laughed. "It's a good plan. You can count on me. Once Marvin is committed, I'm sure he'll help."

Wentworth made no reply to that. He had his own ideas about Marvin Rixson. It was quite apparent that he was the strongman under the Master; that it was he and not Whiting who commanded. If the Spider had not seen Rixson side by side with the Black Police officer whom he knew to be the Master, it would not be hard to believe that Rixson was the Master himself! He frowned. Could he be sure that Rixson had not ordered the officer to fire on the glass panel?

Slowly, Wentworth shook his head. He could not be sure. All that he knew was that only the Master could have known that the recorded voice which sounded was not his own. Any one of the men in the den that day might have ordered the shot, by a single quick gesture.

"Colonel Rice has been wounded," Wentworth said rapidly. "Will you help him dress the wound, Maria? He has to shave also."

Maria Laplante nodded and turned toward an adjoining bath, and Wentworth whispered rapidly to Rice not to let the girl leave the room. Then Wentworth stepped out into the hall and clumped heavily down. "Have you called the commander?" he demanded of the butler. "Well, see that you do at once! A special prisoner from New York City, sent here on orders. Understand?"

The butler showed his distaste for the rough manner Wentworth assumed, but he bowed assent and moved, stiff-legged, to a phone. Wentworth heard the message given to Rixson, answered a few swift questions, then turn back toward him.

"The lieutenant-governor will be here in a few minutes," the butler reported.

Wentworth nodded casually, and fumbled out a cigarette. There were two Black guards outside the front door, huddled in overcoats against the cold. Undoubtedly, Rixson would bring others. If he were suspicious, if he were the Master... Wentworth closed his lips grimly. In that case, they had come to the end of the road!

WENTWORTH'S FACE was impassive as he waited with his automatic ready in an open holster on his hip. No man would have guessed that he knew the fate of the state, his own life and many others hinged on the next few moments. For if things went right—if he and Rice could act swiftly—they might save many men scheduled for death throughout New York, spare countless others who would be slain if the looting started. He had to succeed!

His keenly attuned ears caught the first faint wail of the sirens that heralded Rixson's approach. He was bringing a guard with him all right, but in itself it meant nothing—nothing at all. Wentworth stared out through the steam-clouded window panel of the door, waiting for the first glimpse of the escort

132

Rixson had brought with him. He saw a motorcycle, with a side-car that mounted a machine gun, skate to a halt at the entrance of the drive and wheel about so that its weapon covered the street. An instant later, another motorcycle raced up to the front door and took its position. Wentworth's hand strayed unconsciously toward his gun, but he held it in check. He still could not tell. These might be merely precautions....

Three automobiles raced up the driveway, and from two of them a dozen Black Police spilled, almost before they stopped, and spread out about the grounds with drawn revolvers in their hands. Then Rixson stepped from his sedan, face ruddy with cold, and came deliberately up the steps. There was a frown between his brows and two men, his bodyguard, marched at his heels. Just outside the door, Rixson paused and swung a slow scrutiny over the disposition of his men. He nodded curtly then and reached for the knob. The butler pushed past Wentworth to open the door for him and Wentworth got his shoulders close to the wall.

There was no longer any doubt that Rixson was suspicious. The multiple guards showed that more plainly than any words. Wentworth's gray-blue eyes took on a fierce glint and his lips felt cold and hard against his teeth. It would take more than this to foil his plans! If he had to kill Rixson, take all the Police prisoner....

Rixson stepped through the doorway and his cold eyes swept over Wentworth. "Where is your prisoner?" he demanded.

"Upstairs, commander!" Wentworth made his voice respectful. "He's wounded and the lady is taking care of him."

"Wounded?" Rixson's voice rose. "Who is he, your prisoner?"

Wentworth shook his head dumbly. "They didn't tell me in New York, commander. Only said I'd be shot if he got away." He grinned. "I didn't want to get shot, but the prisoner seemed to. It's not much of a wound."

Wentworth walked awkwardly ahead of Rixson toward the steps, in tune with the lack of precise discipline among the Black Police, and Rixson barked at him. Wentworth stepped aside then, to fall in immediately behind him and in front of the two bodyguards. That was what he had planned and he blocked their following Rixson too closely. Rice knew what to do....

Rixson stopped before the door of the room where Rice was, his eyes frowning and intent. He shrugged, opened the door and stepped inside. The door closed quickly and Wentworth, who had pretended to be about to follow inside, brought up sharply against it. He turned to the two guards.

"Guess he don't want us inside," he said. He stumbled as he took a step toward them, reaching for cigarettes, turned around and swore harshly at his own clumsiness. He had made a noise, and he thought it had successfully covered up the other noises inside—the noise that would be made by a man falling after being struck over the head!

FOR A half hour, Wentworth waited with the two guards outside the door and then Maria Laplante came out. "The commander says you two get your lunch downstairs," she told the bodyguards, then she turned to Wentworth. Her face was very pale and her hands trembled a little. "He wants you inside."

Wentworth thrust open the door for Maria Laplante to

re-enter, then followed her with hand close to his gun, ready for treachery. A man lay on the bed, gagged and tightly bound. Beside him stood another man in Rixson's clothing and with Rixson's haughty air. Wentworth's eyes swung jerkily from one to the other and the man in Rixson's clothing spoke.

"Everything proceeding according to schedule," he said, in a pleasant, resonant voice. "What are the orders, commander?"

Wentworth felt relief loosen all his muscles. It was Rice and his impersonation, even the voice tones, were a much better imitation of Rixson than he had dared to believe possible. Wentworth nodded curtly and reached the bed in a stride, met the angry glare of the captive lieutenant-governor.

"We are taking over the state by this little palace revolution," Wentworth told him quietly. "Help us, and when it's over, you'll be free so far as my men and I are concerned. I made Maria a promise that no harm would come to you."

Rixson turned his eyes haughtily to the ceiling and lay, rigid with his anger. Wentworth turned thoughtfully away. His mind flashed to the heavy guard of Black Police outside the house. It was possible Rixson had given them some special orders as a precaution, but if Rice kept his head… Wentworth scrutinized the colonel, and Rice nodded, frowning.

"I think I can manage," he said.

"You'll have to," Wentworth agreed quietly, "and you will, I know. Come, Maria, we'll accompany Governor Rixson to his den. If we work furiously during the next hour, we will save literally thousands of lives and have a chance to re-establish orderly government."

The peremptory knock at the door whipped them all around, tense with anxiety. A man's voice called out hoarsely, "Hey, commander, you all right? Captain sent me to check up according to orders!"

Rice drew himself up slowly and, as the man shouted again outside the door, he moved steadily forward to meet the challenge. He whipped open the door.

"What the devil are you yelling about?" he demanded harshly. "Yes, yes, I'm all right. I'll be down presently." He turned his back on the Black guard. "Sergeant Whitfield, I'll hold you strictly responsible for the prisoner. He is to see no one, talk to no one. Understand?"

Wentworth saluted crisply while his eyes applauded. "Yes, commander!"

When Rice faced toward the hall again, the Black guard had gone. Wentworth strode forward and thrust Maria into the hall. They went rapidly down the stairs and into Rixson's office. With quick movements, Wentworth loosed the mirror panel. The recording mechanism held no disk and Wentworth rapidly inserted one he had prepared in advance. He whirled back to the others, speaking with rapid emphasis.

"We must get Governor Whiting here," he said. "He will be taken ill and you, Rixson, will be acting governor. You will issue instructions—Maria will show us how it's done—to all the Black police, canceling all their previous orders and rushing them to Albany to put down a supposed rebellion. Meantime, for the same purpose, we will assemble the National Guard units to double the number of the Black Police. When the Blacks are all in one place, we will order them to disband, to turn in uniforms and arms at once. If they refuse…."

Rice's face was pale, his eyes brilliant with mounting excitement. "I didn't know the details of your plans," he said. "It should work! It *will* work!"

Wentworth shook his head. "That's only part of it. You must send out orders, removing every crooked official—mayor and sheriff, you have that power as governor—from office and substituting honest men. Guards of concentration camps must be greatly reduced and, as soon as possible, all the prisoners released…."

"It's wonderful," Maria whispered. "I've been trying to get Marvin to do it, but he was afraid of… of the Master."

Wentworth said quietly, "I also am afraid of the Master! That is our big weakness. We don't know him, or from what point he will strike."

GOVERNOR WHITING protested weakly over the phone but Rice bullied him into coming promptly. He was led into the room where Rixson lay a prisoner, and then made a captive himself. Then Wentworth and Rice went swiftly to work, coding and shooting out orders to Black Police throughout the state, assembling the National Guard. This was the weakness of the Master, that he had always acted through underlings. Even if he appeared in person and tried to block the orders, he would fail since no one would recognize his authority! The record Wentworth had made would help convince any recalcitrant officials….

Within two hours, the first of the companies of Black Police began to roll into town. They were directed straight to the massively fortified barracks the Master had built near Albany and there they found National Guardsmen in command. The men were instructed to turn in all arms for re-issue… Within an hour of their arrival, the first of these men, stripped of all weapons, was being shipped by truck to the concentration camp Wentworth had smashed earlier in the day, and under strong guards of soldiers.

Wentworth was constantly alert at Rice's elbow, awaiting the first hint of opposition. Every possible effort had been made to keep matters secret but with such widespread activity, it was inconceivable that the Master would not learn of it and strike back. Things were moving too swiftly, too smoothly for the Spider not to be apprehensive. Wentworth had little fear of a direct attack on Rixson's house, at least. He replaced the Black Police with an entire company of National Guards, drawn from the citizenry.

A second section of Black Police—three companies this time—was in the barracks being disarmed when the signal corps man Wentworth had installed within the building came into Rice's office at a run and thrust out a radio message.

Rice snatched the message and frowned over it, caught up a list which showed the dispersal of Black Police troops over the state.

"Motorcade estimated at a thousand men coming in from the north," he told Wentworth with sharp excitement. "Speed, fifty miles an hour. No such outfit is shown on this list, and it's contrary to orders. My instructions were, specifically, that they come in small detachments without waiting to assemble."

Wentworth's gray-blue eyes glinted, "That's fully half the Black Police still at large in the state," he said swiftly. "There should be another thousand or so in the south, and...."

The radio operator darted back into the office. "Report from observer in scout plane to the south," he snapped and threw a sheet on the desk, rushed out again.

Wentworth bent over Rice's shoulder and drew in a slow breath. "It's come," he said. "The Master moved even faster than I had dreamed was possible. A unit of a thousand men coming from the south also means that all the rest of the Black Police have been organized for a frontal attack. If we can smash them...."

"They outnumber us heavily," Rice snapped. "We can't hold this house. Have to shift headquarters to the barracks."

Wentworth was smiling with thin, bitter lips.

"Carry on, Rice," he said softly. "Take the prisoners with you. Its open warfare now, but we've at least stripped the enemy of more than five hundred men. I think bombing attacks on the motorcades are indicated. You're in complete command."

Rice rose steadily to his feet, "And you, Wentworth?"

Wentworth's smile tightened. "The Spider will be busy," he said softly. "Carry on!" He strode from the office.

Wentworth slipped down into the basement and entered the secret passageway by which he had once escaped the death trap of the Master. There he set up his small make-up tray, the mirror. Under his deft hands his face rapidly changed its character and became the ominous and sinister countenance of the Spider. He wore the khaki uniform of a captain of the national guard, but he carried a bundle under his arm that contained the brave green cape and the slouch black hat of the Spider.

This was the moment for which he had been maneuvering throughout all the months of battle against the Master and his Black killers. The Master would be fighting in the open, all his forces thrown into one final life-and-death struggle with the powers of law and order. There, in the forefront of battle, the Spider would find him.

CHAPTER 9
DEATH SOUNDS THE BUGLES!

WENTWORTH LEFT the passageway by the garage exit, entered a car and drove steadily in the direction of the fortress-barracks to the north of the city. Motorcycle couriers sped past him in the city streets, as Rice rushed his plans for meeting the power of the enemy. Wentworth had laid no plan of attack. He intended merely to place himself where he could catch a view of both forces of the Black Police and watch them through field-glasses. When he located the Master, he would know how to strike!

He saw that houses were being rapidly barricaded and windows jammed with furniture as protection and he nodded in agreement. Rice had done well to alarm the citizenry. Wentworth switched on the radio in his car and, immediately caught the voice of an official announcer.

"Two regiments of the Black Police have rebelled," the man was saying rapidly. "They are bent on looting the city, on seizing control of the state government for themselves. All citizens are warned to lock and barricade their dwellings, to offer no help to the Black Police on pain of being declared rebels against the government, for which the penalty is death…."

Wentworth nodded in satisfaction. That was shrewd. Now, in extremity, the federal troops might be called in. No, it would never come to that. This effort would stand or fall on the results of the battle today—on the success of the Spider's search for the Master!

He found a vantage point on a wooded knoll within a half mile to the west of the fortress and settled himself down to wait, his binoculars constantly scanning the terrain. He had not long to wait. Damnably soon, in spite of the harassment of bombers, the northern contingent of the Black Police poured over the crest of a wooded hill a mile away. Their cars were wrenched from the highway and, instantly, the men were spreading out in a long line of attack.

Planes were swinging high against the sky and, even while Wentworth watched, the first of them dived to the attack—but *not* against the Black Police! Instead, the swoop of the ships carried them over the fortress, bombs raining down upon the barracks buildings and the concrete walls which defended it! No wonder, the Black Police had come so soon! They had had aircraft to defend them against Rice's bombers!

Plane after plane swooped and dumped its deadly cargo of bombs into the fortification and the advancing lines of Black

Police were opening fire. Wentworth sprang tautly to his feet, a curse on his lips. The southern force was already streaming out of the city streets to attack on the opposite side of the fort held by the national guardsmen! Something had gone woefully wrong. All the rapid plans for blocking the attack—for delaying it—had misfired! In the swift precision of the Black attack, Wentworth saw the swift doom of all his efforts! If the Black Police won, not even the death of the Master would end this tyranny.

One last time, Wentworth's glasses swept the advancing battlefronts and then, behind the southern line, Wentworth's attention centered on an open truck that lumbered in the wake of the attack. A skeleton framework had been constructed over the open body and, from the ridgepole, human figures dangled and swayed with the rough lurching of the truck! Wentworth focused his glasses narrowly, and saw that they were suspended by their thumbs from the framework. Then he saw *who* they were. Their suffering faces were brought into sharp delineation and a tortured cry was wrung from Wentworth's heart. He knew them all… Kirkpatrick, and Nita, his other remaining allies, Sailor Joe and Jackson and Ram Singh, swaying, lurching in that torture rack.

For a moment, Wentworth wavered on the point of hurling himself to the attack. But that was what was intended, wasn't it? Plainly, his allies were being tortured to bait him into the open. That meant the Master was nearby… *The Master!* Wentworth's lips were drawn back from his teeth in a grimace of pain, as he forced himself to continue the search for the commander of these butchers. And he found him—found what he least expected to see....

Within a car, whose heavily armored sides were easily identified, a man rode—one who sent orders ahead by swiftly running messengers, and plainly was the commander of this force. Wentworth's eyes widened incredulously at recognition of that face. It was not possible, and yet the image was there before his eyes, not to be denied.

The commander of the Black forces, the man who must be the Master—*was Marvin Rixson!*

HOW IN God's name had Rixson escaped from the thick guard thrown about his home? But that was not the question now. The problem was to reach and kill him, before his superb generalship smashed the fort and once more loosed upon the people the fury of the aroused Black Police! Wentworth's heart was torn with pain for those tortured friends of his. Curses dripped steadily from his lips, but there was not the slightest chance that he could reach them successfully now—or kill the Master.

As he sent the car hurtling in a long circuit around the battle lines, Wentworth flung aside his uniform cap and dragged down over his head the black wig of the Spider and the wide-brimmed black hat. From the bundle, he fumbled out the long cape of brilliant green and flung it about his shoulders so that its fluttering skirt whipped in the cold wind like a battle flag. After that, he concentrated all his attention on driving.

A concrete strip opened whitely ahead and he sent the car skidding onto it, straightened out for the dash into Albany. A rifleman started from a hidden picket post and began to send bullets crashing at him. Wentworth wrenched out an automatic and laughter burst uncontrollably from his lips, the harsh, mocking laughter of the Spider. One man with a rifle? Did he think he could stop the Spider today?

Wentworth's automatic blasted and was thrust back into its holster. He scarcely needed to see the rifleman hurled, lifeless, back into his covert. Today, the Spider could not miss!

Frantically, he fought to wrench the last ounce of power from the roaring motor. He burst in among the first houses of Albany, without slackening speed. The barricaded entrances of houses frowned at him, but he had not yet reached his goal. He whirled on until he came to a place where homes jostled close together in the shadow of frowning factories, where men slunk like beaten dogs to the cover of slattern walls. These were the people who had suffered most at the hands of the Black Police—who had been torn and tortured to yield up their last dollar for the greedy pockets of the Master.

Where the houses were thickest, Wentworth wrenched the bucking car to a halt and, in one smooth movement, flung himself to the ground and then to the roof of the car. He stood there, both arms lifted against the sky, the green cape swirling and flapping in the winter wind, a banner for victory—or death.

"Now is your chance!" he shouted. "Oh, people, now is your chance to crush the Black Police; to destroy the men who have robbed you; to wipe out the tyrants who have tortured you; to wash out the insult these butchers have put upon free American citizens!"

A few men poked their heads out of their doors. He heard them calling excitedly to each other. Windows were flung open.

"The Spider summons you to battle!" Wentworth sent his deep, ringing voice through the streets. "Come! Every man of the Black Police in the entire state is here today! If you strike now, you can destroy them once and for all! You—" Wentworth singled out a man—"What have you lost to the Black Police!"

Anger suffused the man's face. "Everything, damn them!" he shouted. "My store! My home! My wife…."

"Here's your chance!" Wentworth cried. "Come and drive this car. Drive me through the city streets, slowly, while I call together the victims of the Black Police to rise and destroy them once and for all!"

The man came forward at a jolting run. "Hey you, Taylor!" he shouted. "What are you waiting for? Didn't they kill your boy? Didn't they rob you? Get your gun and come on!"

He sprang into Wentworth's car. "Slowly," Wentworth ordered him. "Slowly, so that people can hear me!"

He dropped to his knees on the roof to brace himself against the jolting of the car, lifted his hands to the heavens. He was a man praying, a bitter Jeremiah summoning the people against the vices of murder and rapine and looting. His voice keened above the rising wind, and everywhere men darted from their houses to stare and some to follow. A half hundred men were trotting behind the car now, grim-faced men with bitter determination in their eyes. Once he had that nucleus, Wentworth knew the mob would grow.

"Americans!" he cried. "Free men! Will you be slaves? Slaves to the Black Police?"

A roar of wrath answered him. No singing for these men. Their hatred was too deep even for fierce hymns of slaughter. They marched in his wake, silent save for the heavy clumping of their feet.

SLOWLY, AT Wentworth's orders, the car described a great circle through the northern limits of Albany. Once, a flying squad of Black Police came upon them and whirled to bring machine guns to bear. Wentworth was on his feet in a single bound and his two guns were in his hands, thundering out death. Four men, Wentworth's swift bullets struck. He had no need to do more. His followers were upon the Black Police, tearing them apart... Afterward, they moved on and they carried two machine guns with them! Small as the victory was, it gave the men courage and unity.

Wentworth halted the march finally and turned to face them from his vantage point on top the car. "To the north of the city," he said, "A thousand Black Police are storming the barracks which is held by the national guardsmen—your friends and mine. If we attack them in the rear, they will crumple. Let nothing stop you until you can join your friends inside that fortress. Machine gunners, forward! Open fire as soon as you come in range of the enemy. Men, march! And the martyred souls of your kinspeople and your loved ones march with you!"

Wentworth sprang down from the roof of the car then and ran to the machine guns. Already, the furious men were in motion, a march as inevitable as the tides. They would follow now where he led… and he would lead them! Right to the Master, and then… Wentworth closed his mind to the memory of those poor helpless friends of his, of Nita, dangling from the ridgepole.

"Forward! Forward!" he shouted.

The light truck of the Black Police, which mounted the two machine guns, lumbered forward. Men were all about it, running, but in grim silence now. They would kill or be killed in that same way. Could the Black Police stand against them? Wentworth's lips twisted bitterly.

Swiftly, the men advanced and burst from the cover of the last houses. The battlefield was spread out before them now, the fortress crumbled in ruins from the blasts of the bombs, but its guns were still going. The Black Police were halfway up the last slope, at a fast charge. Wentworth ranged them with one of the machine guns, turned to face the men behind him.

He flung forward his arm. *"Charge!"*

His order was drowned out in the deep, roaring battle shout of the mob. Wentworth closed his finger on the machine gun's trigger and swung it as a reaper swings a scythe. His bullets sliced the line of the Black Police in half. He saw the white faces turn toward him an instant before they plunged into bloody death; saw the middle of the line ripped wide open as his men leaped forward in the wake of his shots. Whistles piped and swift orders were flung out. Black Police tried frantically to face both ways at once.

Just as the battle was joined, as men leaped with clutching, vengeful hands upon the Black Police—Wentworth heard a bugle blow, clearly and sweet, in the fortress; the rapid pulse of the command to charge and, forth from those crumbled walls poured a khaki column. It was rout for the Black Police. They threw down their arms and fled, and wherever they ran, men leaped and bounded in their wake, determined upon slaughter. Nor would they escape through the city, Wentworth knew. The very children would rise to wreak vengeance.

Nearly a hundred men still ran beside the truck and Wentworth flung them out to meet the guardsmen. Their forces merged and, at Wentworth's shout, a young officer ran forward.

"Take the northern force on its flank!" Wentworth cried.

The man nodded, his face fierce and eager. "Colonel Rice's orders, sir!" he cried, and ran back to his men.

At a double, the united force started for the woods which flanked the Black Police. Wentworth had no longer any doubt of the issue, but his haunted eyes were searching the field. The armored car in which the Master had ridden was gone. The truck with the barren ridgepole was stalled in a ditch, but pitiful figures no longer dangled from its torture rack.

Heavily, Wentworth ran toward the spot, climbed into the abandoned truck. There were bloodstains on the floor. The ropes, that had strung the prisoners up, were severed—but of Kirkpatrick and Nita and the rest there was no trace at all!

A fury of savage futility burned in Wentworth's soul. He had saved the day for the guardsmen, perhaps for the state if he could find and slay the Master, but Nita and Kirkpatrick! What could anything accomplish for him, if they were gone? He stood, shoulders sagging, while the crashing of guns mounted to sudden thunder in the north, continued for a long, long aching moment, and then began to die out. Not victory or death, though they had won. Not that… Victory *and* death; defeat in the hour of triumph….

WENTWORTH TURNED heavily away, started on slow feet toward the fort, the shouting of men turned his head, and he saw some of those he had led rushing toward him. For a moment, hope sprang up in him. Perhaps, they had found those poor prisoners! But it was not that. They babbled of triumph and victory and lifted Wentworth to their shoulders, bore him toward the fortress. They could sing now. Their tongues were loosened in a chant of victory. A sad smile stirred the corners of Wentworth's lips. Yes, he could lead men to triumph over their foes, but his own life was empty and stricken. And the Master still lived. God, yes, the Master still lived….

Wentworth's head lifted with the surge of bitter hatred through his body. He could still revenge! The men deposited him on the steps of the shattered barracks building and cheered him as he went steadily through the door. Here was no place for personal grief, nor time for its assuagement. He must organize an immediate hunt for the Master, and… He thrust wide the door of an office and, instantly, hard hands seized his throat from behind, a gun gouged into his spine!

Wentworth staggered, would have fallen, but for those strangling hands. They were eased when his guns had been taken, but still an automatic gouged into his spine. His wearied eyes swept the room, and something that might have been bitter laughter, or might have been a sob, thrust itself, rock-hard, up through his throat. And he had proclaimed the victory!

Nita was in the room, and Kirkpatrick and the rest. They were bound hand and foot, helpless prisoners against the wall. Colonel Rice was bound by stout ropes to a chair and over him stood two other men who might have been twins for resemblance. One, Wentworth knew, was the liberated Lieutenant Governor Rixson. The other... Wentworth's lips twisted bitterly. The Master had chosen a new disguise, that was all. As Rixson, he had led the attacking force, had entered here of course by some secret way known to him alone. Black Police ringed the room with drawn guns.

Wentworth's eyes swept the room and centered at last on the other woman in the room, on Maria Laplante who stood at Rixson's side. Had she played them false at last, then? Was she the one who had accomplished their overthrow? The Master was talking, easily, softly....

"We meet at last, Spider," he said. "We have met many times before, but never when you knew me. You have fought well—very well indeed. Too bad you couldn't win. I shall have to reconstruct my machine, of course, but that won't be too difficult... when you are dead."

Wentworth was still staring fixedly at Maria Laplante. Her head was carried too proudly for traitor's blood. He swung his eyes from her to Rixson and back again....

"Yes," he said quietly to the Master, "you will be safe enough, once I am dead. There are good men in your force. Men almost good enough and brave enough to be honest, once they are shown the way. Men who might have been great leaders of the people, had they chosen the honest way, who still may lead...."

The Master's eyes sharpened. "Your talking will do you no good, Spider," he said softly, "but I think you'd better be quiet. Other criminals have held you in their power, but because they paused to gloat or to torture you, you have always escaped. You won't this time. I won't even torture you by killing your adherents first. They are but underlings. You the leader...."

The Master's gun lifted steadily and he took deliberate aim at Wentworth's face. "Hold him steadily, men," he said. "Give him no chance to dodge. Good-by Spider! Too bad to lose so worthy an enemy!" He began to squeeze the trigger deliberately, his eyes tight and hard and steady.

"Rixson," Wentworth said quietly. "Now is your chance. Maria...."

The Master wavered. Wentworth dared not look toward Rixson. He held the Master's eyes with his own. "That's right, Rixson," he said. "You can still be the savior of the state. Don't forget that every good reform we have put through has been in your name. The credit can still be yours!"

The Master swore harshly and pulled the trigger. He had delayed an instant too long. In the moment that he squeezed the trigger, Maria LaPlante and Rixson both leaped forward. Their clutching hands wrenched the muzzle of the gun aside. The bullet burned across Wentworth's shoulder and the man who gripped his arm uttered a choked cry as his hands relaxed. Wentworth spun on a heel, his fist striking upward into the face of the Black Police who had held him. Guns were blasting in the room, and there were the shouts of the Black Police. The Master shouted a hoarse command....

WENTWORTH SAW the widening eyes of the man who held him at gun point, felt, more than saw, the blast of the revolver and felt lead tear through his side. But not death itself could have stopped his fist. It jarred home to the man's throat, drove him, already unconscious against the wall. Wentworth sagged to a knee, but he had the revolver now. He twisted about....

In the middle of the room, the Master fought frantically with Rixson and the girl. One of the Black Police stepped forward, as Wentworth watched, and jerked up a gun to smash Rixson's skull. Wentworth's gun blasted, and the Master's man was hurled backward, already dead with a bullet through his skull.

"Maria!" Wentworth shouted. "Cut the prisoners loose!"

The Master's head wrenched toward him, and Wentworth whipped up his and fired in the same moment. And yet, he was too late. The Master ducked and the next moment, Maria held before him as a shield, was backing toward the door. He cleared the way for two more of the Black Police and they threw down on Wentworth frantically. A bullet plucked at his cape and another scored a lock of hair from his wig. They had time for no more than that before the Spider's lead cut them down.

Nita's voice cut sharp across the bedlam in frantic warning, and Wentworth hurled himself face down on the floor. Lead whined past his ear. He twisted... and Maria LaPlante stumbled toward him, pitched across his body. Wentworth wrenched an arm, his head out from beneath her. Down the hall, he saw the

Master just ducking through another doorway. He fired without aiming, without thought, saw the Master stagger and heard him shout hoarsely as he vanished through the opening.

Wentworth fought to be free of Maria's weight, but it was inert across his shoulders, and he was weak... weak. There was a fury in his side where the bullet had struck. He clawed at the floor and, suddenly, the weight was lifted from him. He flung a single swift glance around the room. Rice was free. There were no more Black Police. Reeling, scarcely able to stand, Wentworth fought his way down the hallway toward that door through which the Master had vanished. The fiend could not elude him now....

Wentworth staggered through the door, gun ready, and stared about him in dazed bewilderment. The room was empty! Hell! The secret passageway which Wentworth had deduced must have its exit in this room. If he could find it... Wentworth took a staggering step forward and was suddenly on his hands and knees in the floor. An instant later, warm arms closed about his neck and Nita's lips brushed his cheek.

"He's gone, dear," she whispered. "Lie down. I must bind that wound!"

Wentworth tried to fight to his feet, but he had not the strength. "Be quick!" he whispered. "Be quick. He must die."

He caught his breath then, as Nita set to work on his wound with swift, efficient hands. He was aware of movement in the room, but did not open his eyes. He was thinking swiftly. Something familiar about the movements of the Master in that last swift retreat. He knew the man. He must know him! If only he could think....

Iodine stung his side fiercely, then a bandage tightened about him. The Master. He must know him, must... Abruptly, a great cry sprung from Wentworth's lips. He thrust himself up on an arm, scrambled to his knees. He staggered to his feet, almost fell.

"Some brandy!" he said hoarsely. "Whisky, ammonia. Anything! It must be fast!"

Someone thrust a flask into his hand and he tipped it. The stuff was fiery in his throat. His heart began to hammer with fierce throbs and a false strength touched his limbs. Wentworth laughed, tossed the flask aside. He ran through the door. Men shouted behind him. They were following, but he could not wait. The Master would waste no time. He would make a quick clean-up and fly—or he would return to his own identity and seek to hide under it....

There was a motorcycle in the quadrangle, and Wentworth seized it, ran, stumbling, with it. The motor caught and its forward surge fairly threw him into the saddle. The cold bite of the wind in Wentworth's face helped, but he was reeling. Weak, so damned weak! But he had the Master! He could not escape now!

ACROSS THE jumbled battlefield with its heaped dead, he sped, his green cape kiting out behind him... through littered streets. Everywhere about him were the tokens of victory. Flags flaunted from the windows and women were marching, singing. There were grimmer fruits, too, that dangled from the lampposts—the Black Police who had thought they could escape the wrath of an aroused people.

Cheers....

Wentworth scarcely heard these things. Men were cheering him as he rode, crouched low over the handlebars of the machine. Wentworth drove almost blindly, his eyes strained wide, searching ahead, ever ahead. Finally, he wrenched the motorcycle to a halt and ran at a low flight of steps, pounded up them. The reloaded gun in his hand crashed twice, and the shattered lock yielded under the thrust of his shoulder. He ran along a short hall, blundered in through a door—and then a gun blasted at him from behind a chair.

Wentworth laughed. He did not dodge, nor attempt to charge. He had not the strength. But the gun in his hand leaped and leaped again. Bullets clawed through the flimsy back of the chair. He heard a man scream, saw arms and legs floundering, but the gun in the Spider's hand never ceased to hammer until it gave forth a dry, empty clicking that meant the last bullet was spent. Wentworth went forward then, stumbling, uncertain of his tread, and gazed down on the dead man behind the chair.

The Master had had just time to remove the make-up from his face. His shoulder was roughly bandaged and it....

Wentworth stooped over him and ground against the paling forehead the base of his cigarette lighter. The crimson seal of the Spider sprang vividly to life there. Wentworth straightened, turned heavily away. The strength was going out of him now. He staggered, managed to catch the wall with his hand and leaned there, panting, sobbing for breath. His slow, heavy feet took him to the street, somehow to the motorcycle.

A boy was standing on the sidewalk, staring at him with dilated eyes. "Geez!" he gasped. "Geez! The Spider!"

The Spider managed a smile. "Where's the nearest hospital, son?" he asked hoarsely....

WENTWORTH SAID easily, as he tilted back in a chair in the office of the police commissioner in New York, "Of course, I'd like the claim credit for that kill in Albany—the Master, I mean. The doctors will tell you, I was found unconscious in the streets, and there was no green cape, no face of the Spider, nothing. No, I guess the Spider put one over on us after all, Kirkpatrick. But he still left plenty for you to do...."

Kirkpatrick smiled grimly. "I have plenty to do all right, putting the lid back on the underworld. Rixson is going to make a good man there in Albany, with Maria LaPlante to help him. He'll never turn crook again."

Wentworth shook his head. "If he should," he said softly, "I think some ghosts might well haunt him to his grave. Many ghosts... But seriously, Kirk, we were fools not to have suspected the Master's identity all along. The nub of the whole affair from its beginning was this White Face in the Mirror. That was what sold the plan to its original backers—the fact that the Mirror concealed them absolutely. So the Master had to be a man who could contrive a thing like that, and who better fitted to do that than the man who openly made the mirrors for the Master! That was the cleverest subterfuge of all—and Doctor Kepler almost got away with it. Doctor Kepler, who was the Master in disguise!"

Kirkpatrick was scrutinizing papers on his desk, scarcely listening to his friend, Wentworth. There were so many problems. Suddenly, he uttered a sharp oath and surged to his feet. Wentworth stared at him, saw the white gravity of his friend's face.

"In heaven's name, Kirk?" he demanded. "What is it?"

Kirkpatrick said heavily, "I'll resign! By the heavens, I'll resign first! The damned fools! As if all the world didn't know what a debt of gratitude it owes... Listen, Dick...."

" 'We, the undersigned, respectfully submit, that no drive to wipe out crime can be complete, no citizenry can hold respect for the law, until the greatest criminal of all is brought to justice and made to pay for his many crimes. We submit that this is your task and we urge and, in fact, demand, that you throw every resource at your command into an immediate and thorough effort to find and destroy the criminal who calls himself the Spider!' "

Wentworth broke into laughter, but Kirkpatrick's gravity did not lighten.

"The names on that list command respect, Dick," he said. "I'll either have to do what they demand or resign. And, by God, they can have my resignation right now!"

Wentworth continued to laugh. He picked up the gardenia from the thin vase on Kirkpatrick's desk and wafted its scent to his nostrils. "Why be so disturbed, Kirk?" he said pleasantly. "You've been trying for a great many years to catch the Spider, or find some proof against him—and you haven't succeeded yet!"

Kirkpatrick stared at Wentworth and gradually his mouth corners quirked in a smile. It broadened and he burst into a laugh, and Wentworth joined with him. It was loud and hearty, their laughter. In the outer office, one cop looked at another and grinned.

"Hell, you can't blame them for laughing," he said. "They've won the right to keep on laughing all their lives—after what they've done for this state."

POPULAR HERO PULPS   AVAILABLE NOW:

ACE G-MAN
- ☐ #1: The Suicide Squad Reports for Death $14.95
- ☐ #2: Coffins for the Suicide Squad $14.95
- ☐ *NEW:* #3: Shells for the Suicide Squad $14.95

OPERATOR 5
- ☐ #1: The Masked Invasion $13.95
- ☐ #2: The Invisible Empire $13.95
- ☐ #3: The Yellow Scourge $13.95
- ☐ #4: The Melting Death $13.95
- ☐ #5: Cavern of the Damned $13.95
- ☐ #6: Master of Broken Men $13.95
- ☐ #7: Invasion of the Dark Legions $13.95
- ☐ #8: The Green Death Mists $13.95
- ☐ #9: Legions of Starvation $13.95
- ☐ #10: The Red Invader $13.95
- ☐ #11: The League of War-Monsters $13.95
- ☐ #12: The Army of the Dead $13.95
- ☐ #13: March of the Flame Marauders $13.95
- ☐ #14: Blood Reign of the Dictator $13.95
- ☐ #15: Invasion of the Yellow Warlords $13.95
- ☐ #16: Legions of the Death Master $13.95
- ☐ #17: Hosts of the Flaming Death $13.95
- ☐ #18: Invasion of the Crimson Death Cult $13.95
- ☐ #19: Attack of the Blizzard Men $13.95
- ☐ #20: Scourge of the Invisible Death $13.95
- ☐ #21: Raiders of the Red Death $13.95
- ☐ #22: War-Dogs of the Green Destroyer $13.95
- ☐ #23: Rockets From Hell $13.95
- ☐ #24: War-Masters from the Orient $13.95
- ☐ #25: Crime's Reign of Terror $13.95
- ☐ #26: Death's Ragged Army $13.95
- ☐ #27: Patriots' Death Battalion $13.95
- ☐ #28: The Bloody Forty-five Days $13.95
- ☐ #29: America's Plague Battalions $13.95
- ☐ #30: Liberty's Suicide Legions $13.95
- ☐ #31: Siege of the Thousand Patriots $13.95
- ☐ #32: Patriots' Death March $14.95
- ☐ #33: Revolt of the Lost Legions $14.95
- ☐ #34: Drums of Destruction $14.95

CAPTAIN COMBAT
- ☐ #1: The Sky Beast of Berlin $13.95
- ☐ #2: Red Wings For the Blood Battalion $13.95
- ☐ #3: Low Ceiling For Nazi Hell Hawks $13.95

DUSTY AYRES AND HIS BATTLE BIRDS
- ☐ #1: Black Lightning! $13.95
- ☐ #2: Crimson Doom $13.95
- ☐ #3: The Purple Tornado $13.95
- ☐ #4: The Screaming Eye $13.95
- ☐ #5: The Green Thunderbolt $13.95
- ☐ #6: The Red Destroyer $13.95
- ☐ #7: The White Death $13.95
- ☐ #8: The Black Avenger $13.95
- ☐ #9: The Silver Typhoon $13.95
- ☐ #10: The Troposphere F-S $13.95
- ☐ #11: The Blue Cyclone $13.95
- ☐ #12: The Tesla Raiders $13.95

MAVERICKS
- ☐ #1: Five Against the Law $12.95
- ☐ #2: Mesquite Manhunters $12.95
- ☐ #3: Bait for the Lobo Pack $12.95
- ☐ #4: Doc Grimson's Outlaw Posse $12.95
- ☐ #5: Charlie Parr's Gunsmoke Cure $12.95

THE MYSTERIOUS WU FANG
- ☐ #1: The Case of the Six Coffins $12.95
- ☐ #2: The Case of the Scarlet Feather $12.95
- ☐ #3: The Case of the Yellow Mask $12.95
- ☐ #4: The Case of the Suicide Tomb $12.95
- ☐ #5: The Case of the Green Death $12.95
- ☐ #6: The Case of the Black Lotus $12.95
- ☐ #7: The Case of the Hidden Scourge $12.95

THE SECRET 6
- ☐ #1: The Red Shadow $13.95
- ☐ #2: House of Walking Corpses $13.95
- ☐ #3: The Monster Murders $13.95
- ☐ #4: The Golden Alligator $13.95

CAPTAIN ZERO
- ☐ #1: City of Deadly Sleep $13.95
- ☐ #2: The Mark of Zero! $13.95
- ☐ #3: The Golden Murder Syndicate $13.95